HEART OF STONE

STONEHEART MOTORCYCLE CLUB
BOOK 1

EVIE MITCHELL

THUNDER THIGHS PUBLISHING

This book is a work of fiction. Names, characters, places, incidents, facts, and sometimes random sentences are either the product of the author's imagination or are used in what she hopes is an entirely flattering but fictitious manner. Any resemblance to actual persons, living or dead, or actual events, or locales is entirely coincidental.

Copyright © 2025 by Hendrix House Pty Ltd on behalf of Evie Mitchell; All rights reserved.

ISBN: 978-1-922561-64-0

No part of this book may be distributed, posted, or reproduced in any form by digital or mechanical means, including via Youtube, TikTok, Instagram, Facebook or Twitter, without prior written permission of the publisher.

Editor: Nicole McCurdy, Emerald Edits
https://www.emeraldedits.com/

Editor: Aquila Editing
http://www.aquilaediting.com/

Cover design: Megan Wade
Map design: Evie Mitchell
Images: Deposit Photo

To the discerning readers, who know that steamy reads are an art form.

And to everyone who has taken on responsibility that was never theirs to own.

You've got this.

And to Rooks.

Always.

ACKNOWLEDGEMENT OF COUNTRY

I acknowledge the Traditional Custodians of the lands on which I write, the Ngunnawal people, and pay my respect to elders both past and present.

I acknowledge the continued and deep spiritual relationship of the Australian Aboriginal and Torres Strait Islander peoples' to this land, and their unique cultural and spiritual relationships to the land, waters and seas, and their rich contribution to society.

Always was, always will be.

CONTENT INFORMATION

Please note the following content information include
SPOILERS for this book.

SPOILERS BELOW

Themes

This story contains references to child abandonment,
fostering, poverty, violence.

Includes swearing, and consensual but explicit sexual
scenes.

More information

If you have any concerns with the depictions in this story
or would like further information before reading, please
email Evie@EvieMitchell.com

END SPOILERS

HEART OF STONE

He guards the Stoneheart MC, she guards her heart. When an ice queen mechanic meets a stone-cold biker, sparks aren't the only thing flying.

ANDI

I thought I had my life perfectly tuned - a job I love, an apartment that's safe, and no complications. Then my cousin dumps her three kids on my doorstep and vanishes, leaving me holding the baby–literally.

Now I'm juggling twin toddlers, an infant, and a full-time job while living next door to a motorcycle club. Just what I need - a house full of bikers taking an interest in my business, especially their sergeant-at-arms with his broad shoulders and knowing smirk.

I've spent my whole life handling things on my own, and I'm not about to stop now....right? 'Cause watching Hawk with the kids is enough to make my ovaries explode. And the way he looks at me? My ice queen reputation might be in danger of a serious melt.

HAWK

Being sergeant-at-arms for the Stoneheart MC means handling threats to the club. But the woman living across the street with three kids? She's a whole different kind of danger.

Andi's different from the women who usually hang around the club. She's all curves and attitude, an ice queen mechanic who doesn't need anyone's help. Watching her struggle with three kids she never asked for shouldn't get under my skin. But there's something about the way she holds everything together, the fierce love she has for kids that aren't even hers, that calls to the protector in me.

I'm not looking for complications. The club needs me focused, especially with a new threat breathing down our necks.

But every time that ice cracks, revealing her fire within, I know I'm in for a world of trouble.

Heart of Stone is a steamy, laugh-out-loud motorcycle club romance featuring a fiercely independent mechanic who's never met a problem she couldn't fix, a grumpy, possessive biker who might have met his match, and a small town being torn apart by corporate greed. With elements of forced proximity, found family, and learning to trust, this story delivers heart, heat, and healing in equal measure. If you love curvy heroines who don't need saving, possessive heroes learning to share control, and a supporting cast of lovable bikers who think babysitting is part of prospect duties, this book is for you.

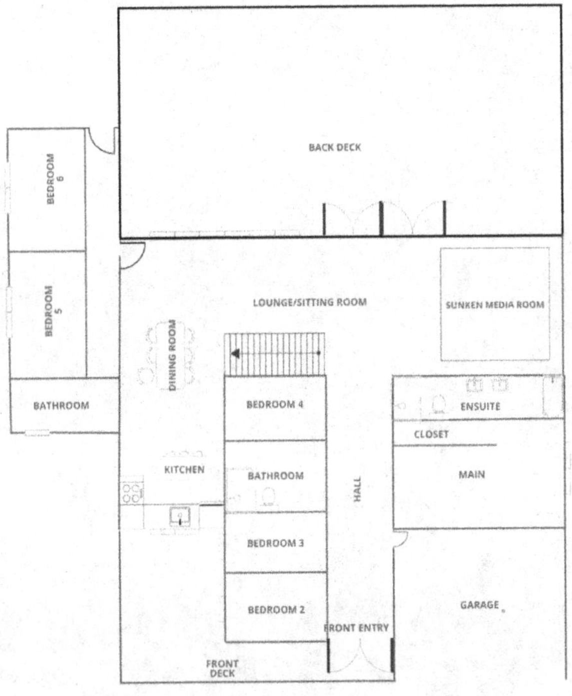

THE CLUB HOUSE

GROUND LEVEL

4 Acres
Land

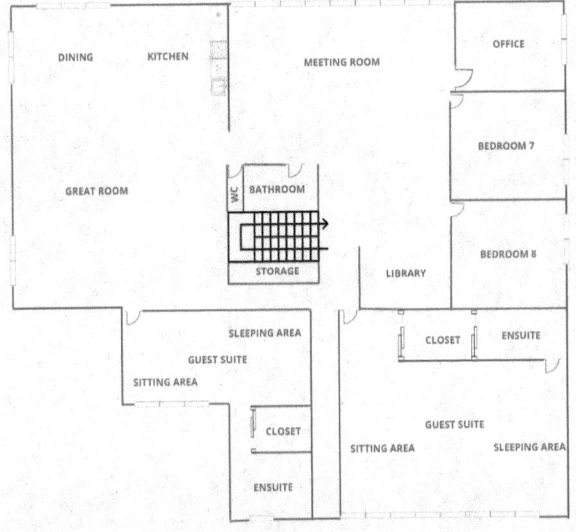

THE CLUB HOUSE
UPPER LEVEL

4 Acres
Land

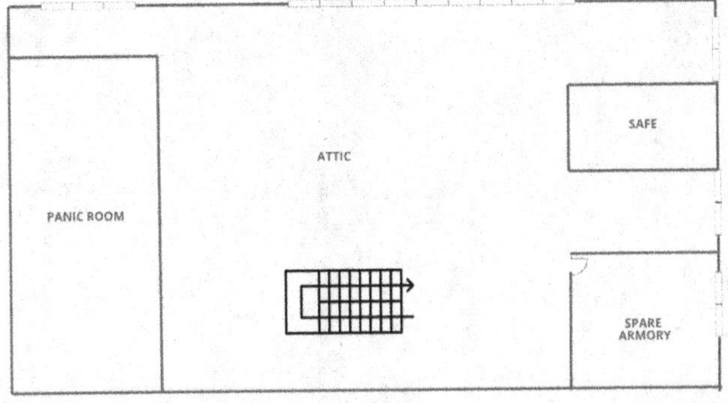

THE CLUB HOUSE
ATTIC

4 Acres
Land

THE CHAPEL

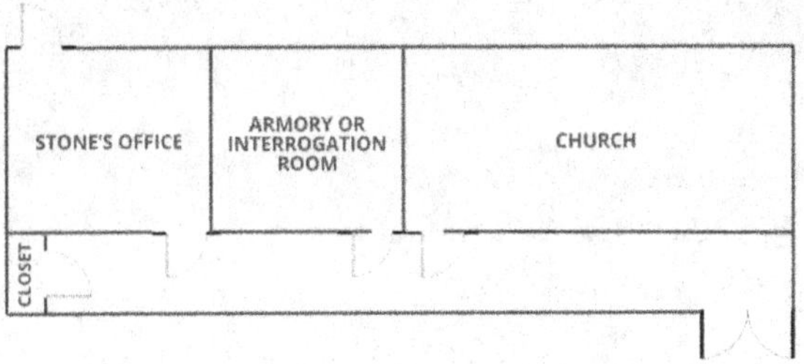

THE BARRACKS
GROUND FLOOR

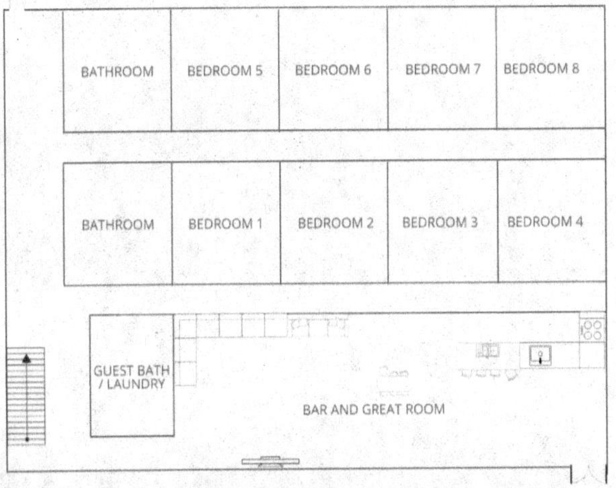

THE BARRACKS
LEVEL 1

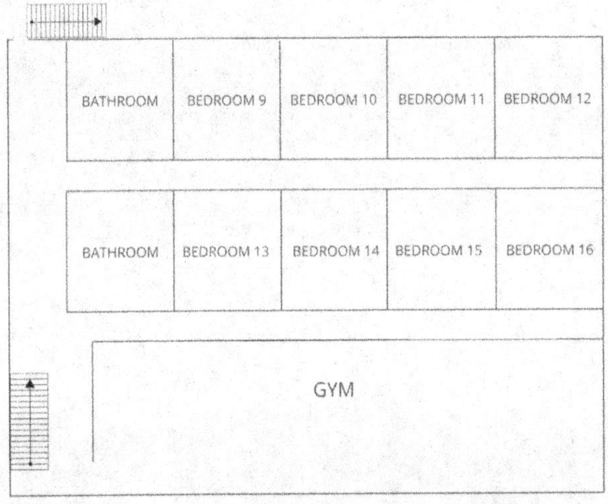

THE BARRACKS
LEVEL 2

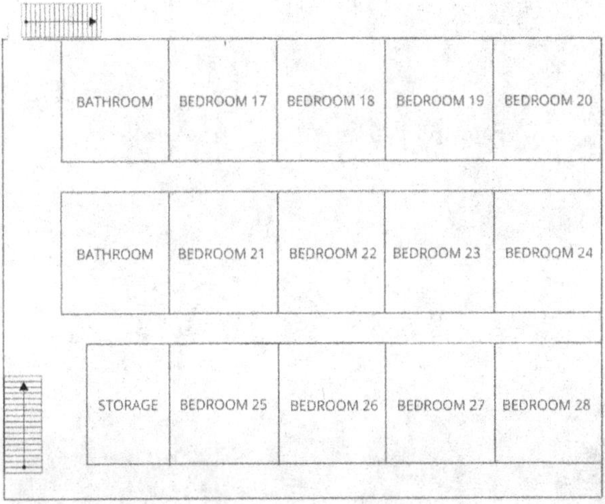

1

ANDI

"I don't understand," I say, adjusting the squirming toddler in my arms. "What are you telling me, Amanda?"

My cousin's voice sounds thin and crackly on the other end of the phone. "You'll need to look after them for another week—maybe two."

I hear someone calling her name in the background as I struggle to process what my cousin has just dumped in my lap.

"But I can't. I have work."

"I know but you can—shit, I have to go," Amanda curses. "Our plane is boarding."

The shock of her announcement evaporates as reality punches me in the face.

"Amanda, wait! You can't do this to me, I—"

"Gotta go! Key to the house is in the letterbox. Rent's due tenth of the month. Kisses to the babies. Bye!"

The call disconnects before I can get another word in. I pull the phone from my shoulder, staring down at the blank screen.

"Fuck."

"Fah!" Abby repeats, smooshing my face between her tiny, sticky hands. "Fah, fah!"

Panic tears through me as I stare at the chaos that my living room has become. The one-bedroom apartment I've lived in for the last twelve months has been perfect for me—a single woman without so much as a goldfish.

For me and three kids? Not so much.

I lean down to set Abby on the floor as the weight of Amanda's decision settles on my shoulders.

"Go play with your sister," I murmur, tapping her on the bottom.

Abby rushes off, her chubby little legs barely able to keep up with her. My cousin has three kids under the age of three: twin girls, Abby and Amy, and a little boy, Adam. The A-Team are cute, I'll give them that, but I'm not prepared for the responsibility of three kids. My apartment isn't exactly kid-friendly.

I run a hand through my hair and over my face, silently screaming. Amanda isn't exactly the most responsible individual. She has a tendency to go off for a weekend, leaving me stuck literally holding the baby. But to do this for a week, maybe more? That is unusual, and I don't like it. I don't like any part of the nonsense I've been putting up with for years.

I blame her current boyfriend. The guy has been around for months, and he is bad news. Baby Adam is an example of that. Instead of Paul being at the birth, it was me holding Amanda's hand. But she's too blind, by love or lust—probably his money—to see what a bad influence he is. But then, I can't blame him entirely. The fact is, she's a grown woman who should know better than to leave her kids to go chase a party.

I guess I should be grateful that Paul is still around. At least he pays child support, unlike the twins' dad, who took off before they were even born. Between Paul and Amanda, they aren't exactly the most responsible parents. They mess up regularly, forgetting they have kids and leaving babysitters to call me when they don't show up at the appointed time. More than once, I've cancelled weekend plans or skipped work just to support my irresponsible cousin and her partner.

I adore my baby cousins, don't get me wrong. I love looking after them and being in their lives. But I'm not their parent. And as much as I hate to admit it, it's becoming clearer and clearer that Amanda and Paul don't consider them their responsibility.

My mind races as I look for other options. There is no way I can call Amanda's mom. My aunt is bad news all over. And my mom? Well, she might be even worse.

An old-school hippie, they both aren't exactly known for their reliability. Between the drugs, the debts, and the drinking—not to mention the deadbeat guys they bring home every weekend—they're not exactly Ms. Reliable.

I run a hand through my hair, listening to the kids play.

Amanda wasn't always like this. We'd been close as kids, just us against a world that wanted to keep kicking us down to the dirt. But somewhere around our teens, we'd begun to drift. I wanted something better than a rusted trailer and a string of men who stayed long enough to drink all your beer but not long enough to pay for another six-pack.

And Amanda... well, she'd chosen differently.

I'd escaped our trailer park on my eighteenth birthday, working my butt off to get my GED and enroll in a course I knew would pay decent money. Being a mechanic isn't exactly the job of my dreams, but the money I make sure as hell makes up for it.

While the kids I'd gone to school with had dreamed of fame and fortune, I'd wished for more than a hundred bucks in the bank, or a regular hot shower that didn't involve a rec center. Add in a night of not listening to sex through paper-thin walls, and all my dreams would have come true.

By all standard metrics, I could consider myself successful. And yet here I stood, a pseudo-single parent, looking after three kids who aren't my own, while my cousin goes off to God only knows where to party with only the devil knows who.

Shit.

I pace as I consider the implications of Amanda's selfish decision. A weekend is different from a week or even two. One weekend in my apartment is tough but doable. A whole week or more? No way. I can't have three kids here. What will I do for childcare? For food? For sleeping arrangements?

The temporary cot will be okay for Adam, but the girls share my bed when they're here, and I sleep on the pull-out couch which isn't the best night's sleep—when I can sleep around a fussy baby and two hyperactive toddlers.

And what about my job? I'll have to look after the kids while I'm at work. There is no way I can bring three babies into the workshop. I am a mechanic, and our workshop specializes in restoring cars and bikes. Hell, we even have the occasional truck. I am good at my job, and people love what I do. I have a little bit of sick leave saved up, but we are in the middle of a big project. I don't want to be the one to cause it to blow out.

Option one: I can call child services and turn the kids over to them, but having been through foster care, there is no way I am going to do that.

Option two: I can try calling Amanda, work out where she is, and drop the kids off, but I have no doubt that would just end up in the same situation within a couple of days. She'd come home, and the kids would be in the house alone. I'd get a call from one of the neighbors or Amanda, telling me to check on them. Alternatively, she'd complain and somehow get into my place, wrecking the joint because I hadn't given her what she wanted. It's happened twice before.

Option three, and perhaps the only one that is actually viable, is to bundle the kids up, take them back to their place, and look after them there until my cousin grows up and comes home to look after her own kids. And since I don't own a car or car seats, we'll have to take the bus.

"Damn you, Amanda," I mutter, beyond exasperated by this situation.

I glance at them, seeing Abby and Amy playing quietly with stuffed toys I bought them.

No one else will care for them as much as I will. Which means this is on me. All on me.

With a heavy sigh I make my decision, glancing at my watch.

It's getting late in the evening, which means the kids need food, a bath, and bed, but there's no way I can look after them tonight and get to work tomorrow. With a frustrated huff, I pull myself together and make mac and cheese for the twins, and heat some frozen breast milk for Adam.

I feed them quickly and shuffle them all into the bathroom for a quick wash before dressing them in pajamas. Assembling their multitude of things—diaper bags, a stroller, blankets, soft toys—I do a quick search on my phone for bus timetables and nearly lose my mind realizing it will take us nearly two hours via public transport for what is essentially a 15-minute drive. But such is the public transport system in small towns.

I live a town over from Amanda. While I might work in Stoneheart, living slightly away from the place I grew up gives me enough distance to carve out a life not tainted by the mistakes of my family.

You might wonder why I don't order an Uber or a taxi—please. The one guy who offers it only works from ten till three during the day, his main customers being old ladies wanting to get to bridge.

With another heavy sigh, I lock up my apartment, adjusting the small bag of items I've thrown into my backpack. The twins are wearing some of those monkey harnesses, which I hate but work when I also have to deal with a stroller as well as carry their stuff. The bus ride itself isn't too bad; I manage to distract them with a movie on an iPad and a pair of headsets. Adam sleeps most of the way, waking occasionally for cuddles, a feed, and a diaper change, which I'll deal with later.

Disaster strikes when the bus finally drops us off a 10-minute walk from Amanda's. The twins, now an hour past their bedtime, are exhausted and not at all willing or interested in walking a step further. It takes some maneuvering, but I manage to slip Abby beside Adam in the stroller and put Amy on my back in a backpack. I move the diaper bag to the stroller's overhang and determinedly shove our way forward as I trudge down the long, broken concrete sidewalk.

Amanda lives in a questionable area, which is no surprise. As a single mom of three whose sole income appears to come from welfare and boyfriends, she has a house whose rent seems dubiously connected to her ability to grant the landlord favors.

I've never asked what kind of favors cause goodness knows I don't want to know.

Once upon a time, this had been a lovely neighborhood with big old trees and quiet small houses. Now it's a wasteland of derelict housing and cleared land.

But there are flickers of life that demonstrate it might be about to undergo a gentle gentrification—the occasional house with new paint and shutters, a car that appears to be a little bit above the price range of the other clunkers around the place. But for the most part, the area is tired, old, and worn with a thin veneer of dilapidation. Old-timers sit on their porches in the summer bemoaning the state of the world while the younger generations trade drugs or guns, or move to the city in an attempt to better themselves.

Maybe one day the town will reclaim its former glory, but for the moment, it isn't the safest neighborhood.

After 10 minutes of pleading, cajoling, and dealing with a disgruntled set of toddlers, we finally make it to Amanda's house. I check the mailbox and, sure enough, I find the key to her house glinting in the dim, flickering streetlight. With a silent curse, I bundle the kids inside and flick on the lights.

It's been over six months since I stepped foot in Amanda's house. Any babysitting had taken place in my apartment. The last time I'd been here was before Adam's birth when I had scrubbed the place from top to bottom and helped her set up the crib because, of course, Paul, the jerk, wasn't interested. But now, stepping inside, I realize that was a mistake. The place is filthy—boxes are stacked here and there coupled with piles of rubbish, dirty laundry, and diapers. The stench of the place nearly overwhelms me, and I gag.

The kids, sadly, take the stench in stride.

Exhausted after a full day of work and this unexpected babysitting gig, I'm beginning to realize the extent of Amanda's problems. The knowledge hits me like a train, barreling over me, crushing me under the weight of responsibility.

There's no way Amanda is coming back, and there's no way I can let these kids go.

Through the door of the house, the twins, exhausted beyond measure, have a meltdown which in turn wakes up the baby, who begins to scream. I drop my bags on the floor, overwhelmed by the mess, the smell, the noise, and the weight of the knowledge that I can't give them back to Amanda. They will need to become my wards. I'll need to take over their responsibility. My life as I know it, as I always imagined it, is about to change.

Freaking out, I quickly bustle around, double-checking that there isn't anything they can get hurt by. I bustle the twins into their bedroom and pop Adam in his crib. I close the door to the twins room, propping a chair under the knob to keep them safely inside.

Tears prick my eyes, and a sick, almost nauseous feeling sweeps over me.

I love them. I love Adam, Amy, and Abby, but I haven't asked for this. It isn't in my plans. I don't have the money to support them. I don't have the apartment or the time, but I'll have to make it work.

I have to do this—for them.

Dreams I have of a house and owning my own business begin to crumble as the weight of my reality rushes in.

I need air.

I stumble to the front door and outside onto the grass of the front yard, falling to my hands and knees in a daze as I gasp lungfuls of cool air, staring up into the dark. My breaths saw in and out too fast, too loud, too wretched. I'm cold and clammy, desperately clutching at the dead and dried grass under my palms. I open my mouth, a scream building in my throat, but nothing comes out.

A sob begins to build in my chest, pain shooting through my body. I'm heartsick for my little cousins who have been abandoned by the people who should care for them. I'm angry—no—furious, at Amanda and Paul. I'm scared, and frustrated, and terrified, and—

"Yo!" The rough call snaps me out of my shock, and I lift my head to see a man staring at me from across the road.

I can just make him out in the light of the streetlamp. He is huge—tall, broad, with thick shoulders and arms, and even thicker thighs. His hair has been cut short—almost to a buzz cut. On his feet are motorcycle boots, his legs encased in dark denim, and his broad chest is covered in a black shirt with some kind of graphic writing on it. But it is his vest that catches my attention. I recognize the patches that indicate a biker.

My boss wears a similar vest, and I know some of the other mechanics have begun hanging around with different gangs or clubs. I can never remember the difference. I keep my head down and do my work, and as long as they pay me well for that work, I don't care what they do in their off time.

My gaze flicks to the house behind him, noting that it is one of the few that appears to be in decent shape—fresh paint, good shutters, good security. It has a massive garage that looks like it has been remodeled recently, the door of which is open, and inside stands a bunch of other guys also watching me. They have busy hands as they huddle around a motorcycle, and I have no idea what I have stumbled into, but I don't like it one bit.

"You good?"

I blink slowly before answering him. "Yeah, I mean... yes. Sorry."

He jerks his head towards the house where the kids' screaming has taken on a new pitch. "You gonna deal with that?"

I blink, surprised and a little thrown. "Sorry?"

"Your kids. You gonna do something about them screaming?" he asks.

I glance back at the house and slowly climb to my feet, running a hand through my hair. "Yeah, I just... I just needed a minute," I stumble over my words, still trying to process everything.

"If you're good, then you better do something before someone calls child services. Kids that small screaming like that."

Isn't that the truth? I think, shaking my head. *They deserve better than a filthy house. They deserve better than being dumped on their aunt's doorstep every now and then. And they certainly deserve better than a belly full of shitty mac and cheese.*

"Yeah," I agree. "Yeah, you're right." I push myself to my feet, dusting my knees and hands. "Sorry, I just... I needed a minute." I repeat, stumbling over my words, still trying to process the events that have led me to this moment.

He jerks his head once more towards the house. "Get your kids."

Your kids.

His words are the slap I need to wake up.

I nod, pivoting on the ball of my foot, rapidly powering towards the house, taking the three steps in one leap and scurrying inside. It would be just my luck if CPS shows up before I can make any kind of rational plan for the kids.

It takes me an hour to calm them down, requiring multiple songs, cuddles, and demands. Once they're in bed, I pull out my phone and text my boss, asking if I can take a long weekend and apologizing for the inconvenience. I explain the issue, and because he's a good guy, he gives me the whole weekend plus Monday at full pay. But then I look around and immediately realize there is no way I am going to be sleeping tonight. The kids' room isn't too bad, but the rest of the house is filthy. I don't know what Amanda has done, but it doesn't look like she has completed any kind of chores or cleaning in at least... God knows when. There is scum and mold growing on cups and plates in the kitchen sink, the trash is overflowing, and the laundry is piled high. It's a miracle the kids have anything clean to wear.

With a deep, soul-wrenching sigh, I search for a pen and paper. I manage to find a pad and sit down at the kitchen counter, beginning to make a list of all the things I need to do and in what order.

There's something reassuring about a list. You can tick off a list. You can add to it. You can see the process, what you need, and what you want all laid out.

I find a modicum of comfort in putting the pen to paper. The action gives me some sense of control, some sense of pride when I finally cross things off. It gives me a goal to work towards that I desperately need when my life is spiraling.

And my life is spiraling right now.

No matter how much I love these kids, they aren't mine. But they are about to be. Their future, their happiness, their lives, it is all about to become my responsibility. I have no idea how I'm going to make enough money to support three kids. The diapers alone are enough to consider mortgaging a house I don't own.

Oh God. Formula. I'll need formula for Adam.

Don't think about it, I tell myself as I add to the growing grocery list. *Just take one thing at a time.*

First things first: a clean house, grocery list, and I'll need a car and car seats.

I think wistfully of my motorcycle back at my apartment, tucked safely away. Of my beautiful bedroom and the little oasis I'd created for myself in my apartment. Of the gorgeous but breakable vase that sits in my kitchen.

The apartment has been mine for three years now, and I have a nice nest egg going with the idea that maybe one day I could purchase something more permanent. But in a single breath of rancid air, that dream has disappeared.

I'll have to work out childcare, and pick up extra shifts to make ends meet. I have no clue how to do that when there are three kids to look after.

God, health insurance. Kids get sick all the time. How am I going to—nope, not now.

A clean house. That has to be my first priority. The house needs to be clean.

So, that's what I do. I start by writing down exactly what I need. It is a long list and ends with ordering groceries—though goodness knows how I'll get them when I don't have a car and there's no delivery service out this way.

There'd be laundry and scrubbing and cleaning and—do we even have any cleaning products?

Jacked up on adrenaline and shock, I start in the kitchen, gagging as I begin to clean from one side to another. I haul garbage outside—garbage that is rotting and rancid, the smell of which is putrid. Condoms, used condoms, are tucked here and there, thrown into corners easily enough that I worry that the girls could have found them.

I toss Amanda's scummy sheets in the washer and uncover an ancient laundry basket. Emptying two of the boxes that had been stacked in the living room, I begin to sort clothing into what is salvageable and what needs to be tossed. Load after load, I begin to make a dent as I clean the house from top to bottom. Here and there, I find stacks of cash and jewelry tucked into little hiding spots. I don't ask questions. Honestly, I don't want to know. I just pile it all up on the kitchen counter, desperately trying to ignore the pit that has begun to form in my belly.

At around 3 AM, I finally put clean sheets on the bed in Amanda's room. Fifteen garbage bags of junk line her front porch, but at least the house is functional, clean, and I have a list of groceries I'll need tomorrow, the top of which includes cleaning products. I have no idea how I'm going to get those grocery items, but I'll deal with that tomorrow. I take a quick shower, scrubbing off the grime, dirt, mold, and filth caking my skin and clothing from cleaning the house.

Tomorrow morning will come soon enough.

2

ANDI

Day one of my new life as a parent to three children starts as any parent would understand: way too early.

I wake to find a child peering at me from the side of the bed.

"Wawy, wawy," Amy says, touching my face. "Potty."

With a groan, I roll out of bed and stumble to my feet, guiding her to the toilet. She does her business, kicking her tiny chubby legs as she chats on about everything and nothing. She keeps gesturing to the bathroom, and I interpret her hand movements as approval for the cleaning job I did last night.

I poke my head into their bedroom and note that Adam is still fast asleep after his 4 AM feed, while Abby has managed to climb out of her bed and now sits on the floor of their bedroom playing with stuffed toys. I didn't clean their bedroom last night, opting to let them sleep, but it's on my list for today after breakfast and shopping.

I take the twins into the kitchen and make them some cereal, watching carefully as they use their fingers to fish out the soggy pieces. It's always been like this, and I'm starting to realize this is less a quirk of a two-year-old and more that they've never been taught how to use spoons or cutlery.

Just another thing to add to my list.

It's Friday, and normally on a Friday, I'd be finishing up my jobs for the week, but today it feels like I'm beginning the rest of my life. I sip some shitty instant coffee I uncover in the back of Amanda's next-to-bare cupboard and start making plans for the day.

First, I need to buy a car. I can't wait. If one of the kids gets sick, I need a way to get to the hospital and cart them around. I'll need to put my bike up for sale. I know it'll fetch a pretty penny, but God, what a blow. That bike is everything I've ever wanted. I worked my ass off for that bike, saving up for twelve months to buy an absolute wreck of a Harley. Over the next year, I slowly restored it myself. Every beautiful inch of it is my blood, sweat, and tears. She purrs like a tiger, flies across the road like a graceful gazelle—delicate but solid.

The bike is perfect in every single way, every decal from the powder blue down to the gorgeous hand-pressed silver with march violets. She's the first thing I ever earned that showed me I was a success, that I could do this, that life could be better. My favorite time of the year is in the middle of summer when I take a week off and just ride her into the sunset. Wherever I land is where I set up camp. I love that. I love the feeling of freedom, of adventure, of knowing that my entire world is the bike between my legs and the open road.

I close my eyes, biting back tears as I realize I have to give up the one thing in my life that has brought me so much joy.

I've had offers on her before—thirty, forty grand. She's a classic, and she's my daily. Forty grand. If I can get that for her, I can't pass up that kind of money when I need to pay for childcare, rent, and a bunch of other stuff I had no idea kids bring with them.

It hurts. It hurts so bad.

Knowing it's better to rip the band-aid off rather than draw out the pain, I dial my boss. He picks up on the second ring.

"Yo, you okay?" he asks, his voice heavy with concern.

Duck has owned the mechanic's shop for close to thirty years. Now in his late sixties, the guy has forgotten more about engines and motorcycles than I could ever hope to learn in a lifetime.

"Yeah," I lie. "Just peachy."

"So, what's going on? Your cousin bail again?"

I make a noise of affirmation. "Yeah, but this time I—" I swallow hard. The words I'm about to say will turn what is in theory a decision into reality. Sucking in a deep breath, I do what I have to do.

"Yeah, this time I don't think it's changing. I'm gonna take custody of the kids."

"Damn. That's rough."

I nod, aware he can't see me but unable to speak around the thick lump of emotion filling my throat.

"What do you need?" His question doesn't surprise me. Duck's a good guy. He might be a biker and a mechanic, but he knows his stuff, and he cares about each of us. He's also the first guy to take a chance on me when I was fresh out of school, and for that, I'm grateful, considering how many other places took one look at my gender and decided I was better off in the office than under the hood.

"I need to sell my bike."

He sucks in a breath. "You sure?"

I swallow. "Yeah."

"What price are you looking for?"

"As much as I can get."

"Got it." I hear him moving around, shuffling. "I might have someone. Let me give them a call."

I push away any regrets I might be entertaining as I watch the girls slurping their milk. "Thanks, I appreciate it."

"Anything else you need? Aside from a shoulder to cry on?"

I chuckle. "You know any good babysitters? Or maybe we could turn the back office into a daycare?"

Duck snorts. "Over my dead body. Don't get me wrong, my grandkids are cute and all, but no one wants them running around during office hours."

I sigh. "Look, I don't mean to be rude, but about our health insurance..."

"Don't worry about it," he says, cutting me off. "You're covered."

I exhale heavily. "Thanks, I really appreciate it, Duck."

"Seriously, don't sweat it, kid. We've got your back. Now, you need a car?"

"How—how did you know?"

"Call me a clairvoyant or the dad of six kids and 18 grandkids. Either way, you're going to need transport, especially if you're thinking of selling the bike."

"Yeah," I admit. "Amanda didn't exactly leave me with the most useful of cars," I say, thinking of the wreck that's been sitting in her yard for the last six months. Even I, as good as I am, wouldn't dare attempt to salvage it. Sure, the parts would be useful, but the car itself is an absolute goner, the engine beyond repair.

"You got anything cheap?" I ask. "Something in my price range?"

"Take the loaner."

I sigh. "I can't, Duck. That's for customers."

"We look after family here," he says, ignoring my protests. "And you're family, kid. Best employee I've had in 30 years."

Tears burn the back of my eyes. I've never had a dad—just one deadbeat after another that my mom brought home. Some were okay, offering me sweets or candy. Others tried to be a dad, disciplining me or urging my mom to take an interest in my life. But the rest? They all disappeared pretty quickly. The longest stuck around for three months; the shortest, a couple of days. I'm not unfair or resentful, never have been. But I regret not having good people in my life, and Duck and his wife, Maggie, are good people. Really good people.

"Thanks," I mutter, unable to convey exactly how grateful I am. "Add me for an extra shift or something. I'll pay you back, I promise."

Duck makes a sound, a cross between amusement and annoyance. "You'll do no such thing. Be here on Tuesday. If you need a sitter, you let me know. Mags would love to look after your kids."

I swallow hard.

Your kids.

That's going to be me from now on. The single mom of three kids.

Jesus Christ, what have I signed up for? What am I getting myself into? I can't do this. Who am I to think I can take over as their parent? I'm no one.

"All right, got to go, girl," Duck says. "I'll get one of the boys to drop around the car."

"Thanks," I mutter. "Oh, by the way, let me text you the address. I'm staying at Amanda's until I can work out what to do about an apartment. Mine isn't exactly child-friendly."

"Got it. Text me the address, and we'll organize the drop-off today."

"Appreciate it. Thanks, Duck."

"Don't mention it."

He hangs up, and I stare down at my phone as Adam begins to make noises in the back bedroom. What the hell am I doing with my life?

It takes some wrangling, but I manage to get all three kids fed, clean, and out the door. Another bus ride across town takes us to one of those kids' stores, where I get all three of them measured up for car seats. A lot of money later, we're off, headed to the real goal: lunch. I feed the twins McDonald's while Adam nurses and I call my landlord.

I moved to a month-to-month lease a few months back, which I never thought I'd need. I guess there's a lot that I never thought I'd need.

I phone in my notice and ask hopefully if he might have any two- or three-bedroom apartments in my price range. It seems my shitty luck is holding as the answer to this is a resounding no.

After lunch, we troop over to the welfare office, where we sit in a long line in a cold, clinical waiting room with slightly flickering lights, waiting to be seen by a case manager. I don't begrudge them the wait, but I get frustrated by the other people in the room who don't seem to understand that juggling three kids while waiting to speak to someone has to be one of the nine circles of hell.

Finally, after three hours, two tantrums, and a ton of snacks, we're ushered into a room.

"Sorry about the wait," the woman says, tucking her grey-speckled hair behind her ears. She has a kind face but no-nonsense eyes, and her brisk manner puts me at ease. This is a woman who's been around the system for a long time, and I can tell with one look that she knows her stuff.

"I'm Robin. How can I help?"

I explain the issue with Amanda and Paul and the filth of the house. Thankfully, last night, I had the foresight to take pictures of the conditions the kids were living in. Robin writes up a report, admitting that, yeah, we'll have to go through CPS, but since I'm already taking care of them and am happy to take on the responsibilities, there doesn't seem to be any reason why I can't continue doing so until the court-ordered mandate is imposed.

"Obviously we'll have to give Amanda the opportunity to make her own case, but the fact that she's currently unavailable—and we've both try calling her—speaks to her situation as a parent." Robin taps a few more keys on her keyboard. "It's not a good situation to be in, but I'm happy to approve you as the temporary guardian until further assessments to the situation can be made."

She hands me a bunch of paperwork—applications that are required for me to be considered a foster parent, classes, and all that stuff. Time I'll have to spend away from them and my job. Time I'll somehow have to find.

"How long will the assessments take?"

She shrugs. "The city is backed up with cases more urgent than yours. Could be a week, could be six months. I'll do what I can."

She explains how welfare payments work and what I'm entitled to as a foster parent to support the kids. There are some discounts, like food vouchers and various items, but the most important thing is health care.

"Are they vaccinated?"

God, I have no idea. I don't even know if they've had their hearing or eyes or teeth checked. Do kids need that this young? I have no idea.

"Don't worry," Robin says kindly, offering me a warm hug. "I'm here to help when you need it. Just know you're doing a great job."

After another long bus ride home, there, sitting in Amanda's driveway, is a car with a young guy leaning against it. I pause in the driveway, watching him with sharp eyes as he continues to text on his phone.

I peg him at early twenties, his face young but with an already hardened look to it. He wears thick boots, dark jeans, and a faded green shirt. Tattoos decorate one arm, and I get the impression that while he's lean, the kid knows how to handle himself.

The same patches that decorate his leather vest match the vest Duck wears. Stoneheart MC.

Duck tried to explain it to me once when I asked about it, and I think I understood a little bit. The club is like a brotherhood filled with guys who live on the mountain. They respect the law insomuch as they abide by some of it, but they do whatever they want otherwise. If it doesn't hurt others, they don't see a problem with why they shouldn't be doing it.

I just assume that means everything they do is illegal, but at the same time, I don't really care. Duck is a great boss, and none of the bikers or their women who come in with their motorcycles or cars ever really give me trouble.

And sure, occasionally there's one that catches my interest—I'm only human after all—but I never do anything about it. I have enough trouble in my life without adding a guy into the equation. If I need to scratch an itch, I go bar hopping.

You don't mix business with pleasure, and you certainly don't get involved with people from work.

The guy looks up from his phone, then nods in my direction. "Duck sent me," he says, tipping his thumb towards the car. "Said you need this."

"Couldn't spare one of the guys at work or something?" I ask, painfully aware that I must look haggard, exhausted, and more than a little frazzled.

It's been a long day. You're allowed to have shitty hair.

The kid shrugs at my question.

"Well, thank you." I let go of the twins' monkey backpacks, allowing them to run up the driveway and head for the door. "Appreciate your time."

The guy nods, reaching into one of his pockets to pull out some keys.

"Here," he says, handing them over, "Duck said to tell you to give him a call if there's any issues. Otherwise, he'll see you Tuesday."

He glances pointedly at the two girls currently pounding their little fists on the front door of Amanda's house. "You need a hand with anything?"

I shake my head, more than slightly amused that he even offers. "No, but thanks. I really do appreciate it."

"No problem."

I glance around, noting that the kid doesn't have a ride.

Shit.

"Hey, how are you getting back?" I brace myself, hoping against hope he's got it covered.

He jerks his head to the house across the road. "I'm covered."

I turn, taking in the numerous cars and bikes gracing my neighbor's front yard. Their garage is open once again, and a multitude of people are standing inside, drinking, eating, and laughing.

For a brief moment, I want to dump the kids and walk across, grab a beer, and lose myself in that—in the carefreeness of them, in the way they seem to have no responsibilities, no worries.

Instead, I turn away, determinedly pushing the stroller toward the house. "Thanks again. Come on, kids, let's go inside."

The weight of responsibility settles on my shoulders once again. The courses I need to take, the CPS hoops to jump through—it all feels overwhelming.

Amy glances at me as I lift the stroller up the stairs. "Wawy, wawy," she says in her determined little voice. "Noodles."

I sigh, adding yet another thing to my to-do list.

"Mac and cheese," I agree, forcing a smile. "Let's get you guys inside and fed, hey?"

I go through the motions with them—feeding the baby, changing him, feeding the girls, washing them, tucking them all into bed and watching them fall asleep after two-and-a-half stories.

The thought of eating mac and cheese turns my stomach, so I do what any sane person would. I throw on a load of laundry then pull a six-pack from the fridge—one of the only things Amanda actually stocks regularly—order a giant pizza, and grab the baby monitor before going outside to sit on the porch.

It's there, with a beer cracked, that I sit in the dark, watching as the house across the street slowly grows wilder.

Motorcycles had rolled in throughout the afternoon and into the evening, bringing with them a parade of scantily clad women—some young, some old, some ancient. A few sport their own patches and vests, proudly declaring themselves "Property of" this guy or that.

My pizza arrives and rather than retreat inside, I lounge on the porch, nursing my second beer and demolishing my hot-as-hell pizza. The steady rhythm of the twins breathing through the baby monitor is background noise to the party across the street, their music thumping loud enough to rattle my teeth.

As the night wears on, I duck inside twice to tend to Adam—feeding him, changing him, and tucking him back into bed. He's so damn tiny, all scrunched-up face and miniature fingers and toes. He came early, staying in the NICU for two weeks before they let him come home. The girls are just as vulnerable, with Amanda's dark hair and their dad's big blue eyes, whoever the hell he is. Each of these kids is precious beyond words. I run my hand over their hair, planting kisses on their foreheads.

Part of me aches to be across the road, to lose myself in one final night of freedom, but I know this is where I belong. These are my kids now. The moment Amanda bailed and I stepped up, they became mine. And I'll be damned if anyone tries to change that.

I still need to figure out what the fuck I'm doing with my life, but whatever comes next, it'll revolve around these three. With Adam settled, I wander back out to the porch, plopping down and picking up my beer.

The front yard is a goddamn disaster zone. Weeds sprout defiantly from the dirt, while scraggly shrubs fight a losing battle against rusting cans and other trash. Smack in the middle sits Amanda's car, a rusted-out hulk missing its tires and muffler. I took a crack at fixing it one afternoon, only to discover she hadn't put oil in the damn thing for three years. When she finally did, the engine blew itself to kingdom come.

Cleaning up this mess is next on my endless to-do list. Tomorrow, I'll get those car seats fitted, which means I can finally haul the kids to a real grocery store. No more mac and cheese and stale cereal.

Christ, has Amanda really been living like this? The kitchen is a wasteland—three sad containers of frozen breast milk, half a carton of regular milk, and some bottom-shelf cereal. Oh, and enough beer to drown a small army. Even the freezer is stocked with vodka instead of kid-friendly treats like ice cream or popsicles.

I pull out my phone and start hunting for local childcare centers, praying I'll find something—anything—that's both taking new kids and won't bankrupt me. Fat chance of that. Even with government assistance, affording decent care seems about as likely as winning the lottery.

I'm beyond frustrated, pissed off, and miserable, which is probably why I react the way I do when a biker parks on the sidewalk, yanks off his helmet, and tosses me a wink. I find myself raising my hand in greeting.

"You should come join us," he says, nodding towards the rager across the street.

I size him up, taking a long pull from my beer. "Maybe." I shrug. "Not exactly dressed for a party, though."

His eyes rake over me, and I feel that look deep in my gut. My thighs clench involuntarily. For once, I'm glad to be sitting down. I know I'm not exactly most guys' idea of eye candy—too muscular, broad-shouldered, with tits, ass, and thighs that are more Amazonian than pin-up girl. My waist nips in a bit, but most of my shirts don't do me any favors. At just shy of six feet tall, with a job that leaves me bruised and grease-stained more often than not, I'm not winning any beauty pageants.

My dating history is a joke. Three boyfriends, each one a bigger disaster than the last. The first cheated, the second bailed when I wouldn't indulge his kinks (sorry, but playing pony with a tail butt plug just isn't my idea of a good time), and the third—well, he took the cake. Cleaned out my accounts, pawned everything I owned, and vanished. I was more pissed about losing my tools than I was about him leaving. Asshole.

"You look just fine to me," the biker says, giving me an appreciative once-over that, I have to admit, strokes my ego a bit.

I hesitate, fiddling with the label on my beer as I weigh my options. If I bring the baby monitor, I could theoretically pop over, check out the scene, maybe grab another drink and shoot the shit for a bit before heading back if the kids need me.

In the end, though, I do the responsible thing. I raise my beer in a salute and shake my head, smiling ruefully.

"Thanks for the invite, but I'm good here. You have fun, though."

He grins and shrugs. "Suit yourself. Offer stands if you change your mind."

I watch him walk away, feeling a complicated mix of regret and relief. With a heavy sigh, I take another long swig of beer and settle in to let the music wash over me from afar.

Maybe in another life I'd accept.

But not this one.

3

HAWK

The woman has fallen asleep.

Around me, music pulses loud enough to rattle the panes of the empty houses flanking my own. The brothers are drunk and rowdy, gunning their bikes and trash-talking on the front lawn. But the noise is nothing to the woman asleep on her porch across the street.

My jaw clenches, my fingers tightening around my beer bottle as I stare at her. If she's out here, then who the hell is looking after her kids?

Not your problem.

I'd clocked her earlier in the evening and half-expected her to come across and ask us to turn the music down, but she'd sat on her porch, drinking her beer, eating her meal, and then falling asleep.

If she's that tired, she should be inside in bed, not out on a porch where any man and his dog can take advantage.

I force myself to turn away before I do something stupid, like stalk across the road and shake some sense into her.

I turn back to the party, watching as women dance in the garage and on my lawn, trying to entice my brothers, whose hands linger on their bodies appreciatively. Here and there, people are fucking—and I have no doubt all of the rooms inside are taken up by at least one, if not more, couples.

"Great party." Duck hands me a fresh beer.

I set my empty aside and accept the cool bottle with a muttered thanks. The old-timer leans against the rail beside me, settling in. Duck's been with the Stoneheart Motorcycle Club for over forty years—patched in as a punk-ass twenty-year-old. The only time he hasn't worn the colors was during his service in the army.

He looks a little like Santa with his beer gut, white hair, and gray-white beard. And while he might be the one who dresses up to delight the club kids at Christmas, I've been in more than one tangle where he's saved my ass.

A good brother to have at your back. A better one to train you on how to become the new sergeant-at-arms.

He eyes the patch on my chest, the one that declares my position in the club. "How's that feel?"

"Fucking good," I admit. "How's *that* feel?" I tilt my bottle toward the space where my patch used to sit on his cut.

"Fucking good," he echoes with a chuckle. "I'm old, Hawk." He claps a hand on my shoulder.. "Club chose you, and I've taught you all I know. You'll do well by it." He chuckles again, leaning back against the rail. "Besides, I don't have the patience to deal with the prospects."

"Speaking of, how's the new kid working out?" I ask, referring to his latest apprentice. Duck owns the only garage in town—a profitable venture thanks to his stellar reputation and side hustle restoring classic vehicles. Last I heard, there's a waitlist of rich pricks from out of state wanting Duck to give their cars a once-over.

Duck grimaces, shaking his head. "He's not. Doesn't want to listen to the girl. Shame. She's a good teacher and knows her shit. Best employee I've ever had."

I cock an eyebrow. "You keep saying that, but every time I come in, this mythical woman seems to be missing in action. I'm starting to believe she's a fabrication of your imagination, old man."

Duck nods toward the house across the road where Ms. Parent-of-the-Year nominee sleeps soundly on her porch. "Hard to say that when you're living across from her."

I blink, my brain slow to process. "*Her?*"

Duck nods. "Yep." He lifts his beer, taking a long drag.

I glance back across, taking in the house with new eyes.

The neighborhood isn't exactly up and coming. Filled with abandoned houses and questionable characters, it doesn't scream "place to raise a family." In fact, if I hadn't seen her walking into the house carrying a baby and wrangling two toddlers, I'd have assumed the place was abandoned. A wreck of a car sits up on bricks, rusting gently in the front yard, fitting right in with the trash that pockmarks the dirt-and-weed lawn. The house itself has seen better days—with its sloping roof, broken gutters, and peeling paintwork.

"Your best employee has three kids and lets her house look like that?" I ask, wondering if she's blowing the old guy. I've never once seen Duck stray from his old lady, Maggie, but stranger things have happened.

Duck snorts. "Hell no. The girl is neat as a pin. You know why the garage looks so good? All her." He elbows me. "Nearly as anal as you are about that shit."

I point my beer at her yard. "Evidence suggests otherwise."

"That's her sister's place. Or is it her cousin's?" Duck pauses, then shakes his head. "Anyway, she's the one with three kids—all under three, mind you. Twin girls and a boy. Scatty as a bag of dropped marbles. Dumps the kids regularly to take off with different jackasses."

"And your girl picks up the pieces?" I ask, putting it together.

"Yep." He makes a frustrated sound. "She's going for custody this time. The mother disappeared two days ago. Far as I know, she hasn't heard a peep from her since." Duck squints into the dark. "She still out there sleeping?"

I glance across the road, taking in the sleeping woman with new eyes. "Yeah."

The word feels heavy, sticking in my throat as a touch of guilt twists in my chest. I can't see her face from here, but the memory of it lingers—the weariness in her eyes, the quiet strength beneath it. I'd been so quick to judge, so certain I had her figured out. But now the edges of that certainty blur, leaving me unsettled. She's not the person I assumed she was.

Fuck. Maybe Axel's right and I am getting jaded.

Duck shakes his head. "Shit for her. Gonna be shit for me if we can't make this work."

I raise an eyebrow. "You're gonna fire her?"

He shrugs. "Might not have any choice if she can't make the hours work. Three kids on one wage as a single parent? And they ain't school-aged yet. Childcare is expensive. I like her—she's a hard worker, good at her job, committed. But I got a shop to run and other employees I have to pay too."

It's all bluster. I know Duck, the man is a fucking pushover. If he likes her, he'll do whatever he can to keep her on.

I lift my beer, taking a long pull as I consider her. "What's her name?"

"Brandi—with an 'i.'"

I snort, beer burning my nostrils as I cough. "You're shitting me."

It was a long running joke that I'd called my first bike

Brandi. Loved that thing before it got wrecked after a jackass backed into it in a parking lot.

Fuck, I missed that bike.

Duck thumps me on the back. "No shit. Girl goes by Andi, though. With an 'i.'"

I glance back across the street, considering her. She sleeps, illuminated by a small light on her porch. Her head slumps to one side, her hands resting in her lap. Her ponytail has slipped, letting dark brown-red hair fall over her shoulder and down her breast. She wears a simple white shirt with dark-wash jeans, but that shirt is working harder than the devil to highlight her assets.

Curves. Curves for fucking days. An abundance of them that—had we met in any other circumstance—would have had me working to get her under me.

But I have new priorities now. Ones that don't include getting involved with a woman and her kids.

"Nice girl," Duck says offhandedly. "If you like curves, she's a looker, that's for sure."

"No man?"

He shakes his head. "Never once got a hint of one sniffing around. Though the guys at the shop have tried." He chuckles. "She puts them in their place quick smart."

"She into girls?"

"Doubt it. Doesn't check out the girls like she does some of the guys when they wander in. Never does a goddamn thing about it, though. Says a lot about her that she doesn't shit where she eats."

I lean against the porch railing. "You like her."

He nods. "Thought about bringing her into the club for a while. She'd make someone a good old lady. Smart, organized, helpful, knows how to keep her mouth shut. But she's cold—like ice. Puts up a wall to anyone trying to get close." He makes a disgruntled sound in the back of his throat. "Shame. I expect it'll be a while before any man bothers to see if she's worth the defrost."

"And is she?"

Duck chuckles. "You interested?"

I nurse my beer, watching the woman sleep as I dissect Duck's assessment of her. Good worker, clean, dedicated, responsible.

Might be a problem.

"Not in that way." I glance at him. "How responsible we talking?"

He strokes his beard, considering. "I see what you're getting at, and you may be right. Too responsible. She hears or sees something—especially with those kids in the house—she might call it in, get us on someone's radar."

The club chose this location for a reason. The area is quiet, filled with dilapidated housing and tenants who ignore any after-dark dealings.

The house itself has a small frontage—but some previous owner blew out the back end, adding a bunch of rooms and space. The backyard stretches the length of the block, complete with a carriage house we'd turned in the Chapel, a barn we'd converted into barracks for the prospects and visiting members, and an additional set of sheds. It had been a farmhouse back in the day before the city sprang up around it. After the financial crash in the early '00s, our small town rapidly decayed as families defaulted and the local industry collapsed.

We're just beginning to pull ourselves out of the mess.

It was a perk–or curse, depending on the day–of the job that I was tasked with protecting the club house, chapel and grounds. Free rent was always welcome, the headaches that came with cocky club members not so much.

Duck clucks his tongue. "Though, in fairness to her, she's not said boo about the stuff she sees at the garage."

As sergeant-at-arms, it's my responsibility to consider any and all threats to the club—and neutralize them before they become an issue.

And little Ms. Responsibility has just become a threat I need to handle.

ANDI

I wake to a kink in my neck, drool on my cheek, and the sounds of a fussing baby.

Groaning, I rub my neck and straighten. Full darkness has fallen, and I can tell the hour is late based on the movements of the crowd partying across the street. The music pounds out of speakers, no less loud than it was hours ago, but the crowd moves to it differently. They no longer stand in clumps laughing and talking and occasionally dancing—now they move in time to the beat, grinding against each other.

I glance down at my watch, noting it's just a fraction before two in the morning.

Ugh.

Yawning, I scrub a hand over my face, pick up the baby monitor, and head inside.

The small rental has only two bedrooms, which means three kids plus an adult is a tight squeeze. After last night, when he woke the twins twice, I moved Adam's crib from the twins' room to the main bedroom, tucking it beside my bed. I'm not sure why Amanda didn't have him in her room, but it sure makes for a quieter night.

Adam kicks his little legs when he sees me, his chubby cheeks pulling into a gummy grin. I grin back, chuckling at the smell emanating from his crib.

"Pee-youh!" I whisper, waving my hand in front of my face. "Stinky boy. Let's get you cleaned up."

Once his diaper is changed, I lay him against my chest and poke my head into the twins' bedroom, finding them fast asleep.

They might look identical, but they're wildly different kids. Amy sleeps sprawled out, a toy clutched in one hand, while Abby is curled into a tiny circle, her blanket tucked under her chin.

Grateful Adam hasn't woken them, I make my way into the kitchen, cooing softly to my little cousin.

"You ready for some milk, little man?" I ask, bouncing him on one hip as I pull the third-to-last pouch of breast milk from the freezer. "Let me defrost this, and—"

The lights in the house blink out, washing us in darkness. Unfortunately, the music across the street continues to pound, which tells me this particular blackout is isolated to us.

"Shit."

Adam gurgles in agreement.

"It's fine," I say lightly, pulling my phone from my pocket and switching on the torch. "It'll just be a faulty fuse. Let's check it out."

I carry Adam outside to the fuse box, and by the light of my phone, I attempt to reboot the power to the house.

Nada.

I'm not sure which diligent electrical employee is up at bumfuck o'clock on a Saturday morning, but it looks like I should have prioritized sorting through Amanda's bills instead of spending the day at CPS.

"Damn," I mutter, adjusting Adam in my arms. "This is fine. The hot water will still work. It'll be cold showers tomorrow, but we should be fine now."

Back in the kitchen, I twist on the hot water, only to find a small drip squeeze out before fading to nothing.

They've shut off the water too.

"What the hell, Amanda? Who did you piss off at the utility company? Okay, deep breath, we can work this out," I say to Adam, starting to feel panic claw up my throat. "How long does it take for milk to defrost?"

Adam chooses that moment to squeal, beginning to gnaw on a tiny fist. He screws up his face, and I know we're about to descend into World War Three.

Damn.

"Does your momma have a grill? I could boil water. Or maybe we could make a fire. Or maybe—"

A loud crash followed by laughter interrupts me.

I glance over at the door as Adam continues to fuss.

Could I? No. That'd be a terrible, horrible, no-good idea.

Adam's little body jerks, his face turning red as he screws up his brow.

"Okay! Excursion time!"

I grab the baby monitor and tuck it into the pocket of my cutoffs. Snagging his bottle and the frozen milk, I lock the house tight and power-walk across the street.

The drunks in the front yard don't pay me any notice. The two young guys stationed near the bikes, however? Yeah, they clock me before I even hit the sidewalk.

"Yo," one of them says, stepping into my path. "You can't bring a baby in here."

I tilt my head back, wondering what I did in a past life to deserve the misfortune that's dropped on my head over the last three days.

"Hi, I'm not actually trying to bring a baby to the party— that is—I mean—" I juggle Adam and tug the bottle from under my arm. "I need to borrow your microwave. Or stove. Or kettle. It won't take long—just a few minutes to heat up his milk."

The biker kid with his Prospect patch stares down at the bottle like it holds shit.

"You can't do this at your place?"

I shake my head. "Ah, no. Appears there's some kind of power issue."

Adam chooses that second to let out a screech, letting the world know exactly how hangry he is.

"I'll pay you," I say, desperate to avoid the forthcoming meltdown. "Please. It'll just take ten minutes to—"

"We all good here?" A hand settles on the curve of my lower back.

I twist, holding Adam close as I stare up into the eyes of yet another biker—the same one who'd yelled at me when I had my freak-out.

Oh, shit.

His glower makes it very clear he isn't pleased to see me.

"You," I murmur, my chest tightening.

He wears dark, worn jeans, thick boots, and a once-black shirt that's faded to grey. On his chest sits a leather cut, the patches just visible in the dark. They read *Stoneheart MC, Sergeant at Arms,* and *Hawk.*

I've been around enough bikers at the shop to know what those, and the other patches I can't yet make out, mean— this guy is club through and through.

A flush burns hot under my skin, the memory of him catching me on the front lawn crashes back with humiliating clarity. He'd seen me—raw, unsteady, completely unraveling. My stomach twists with shame and embarrassment.

No one sees me so vulnerable, so uncontrolled. They can't. I don't let them.

But he did. And I hate that he did.

I can't meet his eyes, not fully. Not when I can still hear the sharp edge in his voice and feel the judgment in his gaze. I shift Adam in my arms, a weak distraction from my discomfort.

Hawk's jaw clenches, his gaze dropping to the baby in my arms.

"You bringing a baby to a biker's party?" Hawk asks.

I shake my head, stepping away from his hand and moving backward to give us space.

"No," I reply, trying to get a grasp on my emotions. "I'm bringing a bottle to my neighbor in hopes you might be able to warm it up for me." I hold up the frozen milk. "I just need to zap it in the microwave for a few minutes, otherwise he's gonna freak."

Hawk looks from the frozen bag to Adam, then meets my gaze.

"You can't do this at your place?"

I swallow. "It appears we're without power. Or water."

A muscle jumps in his jaw, and for a beat I think he's going to refuse me. "Follow me."

Practically wilting with relief, I trail him, trying to keep my shit together as Hawk picks his way through the crowd, ignoring the revelry around us.

He might be immune to it, but I can't ignore the multitude of sins playing out before me. Music swirls around bodies grinding into each other—some naked, some barely clothed. I watch as a couple fuck openly, his dick sliding into her pussy.

I duck my head and cover Adam's eyes, protecting him from seeing something that he absolutely shouldn't at this age. Or any age. Maybe I can convince him to be a monk cause goodness knows I'm not equipped to have a conversation about sex with horny teens.

We walk up the porch steps and enter the old farmhouse. I have a moment to appreciate the high ceiling and gorgeous wood flooring before we're sucked back into a crowd—one that's less loud but more decadent than those outside.

The music is dimmed inside, and I whisper a silent prayer of thanks that I don't have to worry about Adam's hearing.

We walk down a long hall, and I smell the muddy scent of weed, sweat, beer, and sex.

We pass rooms full of people chatting, laughing, arguing, and—in some instances—fucking.

I'd assumed the house was only slightly larger than my own since its street frontage isn't large even though it has a second story, but I'm proven wrong. The house stretches backward for what feels like forever, merging a new addition with the old farmhouse.

We enter the kitchen, and I find I don't quite know where to look. Half-naked women lounge across counters while men stand around shooting shit.

"Oh! A baby!" one of the women squeals, bouncing her way over to us—her breasts echoing her movement. She's a striking redhead, her hair a cascade of fiery curls streaked with hints of silver, the kind of wild, unapologetic hair that seems to match the energy she radiates. Fine lines frame her eyes and mouth, softening the bold red of her lipstick and the playful sparkle in her gaze. Freckles still dust her cheeks, a lingering trace of youth on a face full of warmth as she beams down at Adam.

Adam squeals happily—forever enthused by attention.

I smile awkwardly, holding him as the gorgeous woman claps in front of us, making silly faces.

"Ginger, get your ass back here," one of the bikers barks. "She's baby-obsessed. I swear."

She laughs, tossing her hair. "Just one more? Please?"

I blink, surprised that with a body like hers, she could have any kids.

"No. We're both too fucking old," the biker says, holding his arm out for her to slide under.

"Microwave is there. Use it," Hawk interrupts, crossing his arms over his chest.

I do as I'm told, quickly warming Adam's milk.

"Oh, did your microwave break?" Ginger makes a moue of sympathy. "That sucks. You need me to take him while you do that?" She wiggles her fingers at me.

"Ah, thanks but I think he's okay."

The biker with his arm wrapped around her sighs heavily. "You gonna talk babies all night or pay me some attention?"

She elbows him playfully. "Maybe. Unless you have a better option for me?"

He pulls her into him, catching her mouth with his for a deep kiss.

I flush, glancing away as I watch the timer countdown.

What the hell was I thinking coming over here? And with Adam? I'm definitely not about to win any guardian of the year awards.

The deep rumble of Hawk's voice slides over my skin, low and commanding. Before I can protest, heat radiates against my back, his big, tall body closing in behind me, crowding my space.

I twist, heart thudding, but he's already moving, those rough, capable hands brushing the bare skin of my arms as he carefully slips Adam from my hold. His touch sends a ripple of awareness cascading through me, tingles racing down my spine, leaving goosebumps trailing in their wake.

"No, that's okay. I can—"

"I got him." His voice brooks no argument, but it's not harsh—just steady and sure.

Hawk shifts Adam with practiced ease, cradling him close against his chest, the baby's fussing quieting almost instantly. Adam blinks up at the biker, his tiny hands curling against Hawk's leather cut.

"Hey," Hawk murmurs, the softness in his voice a contradiction to the hard edges he's shown me up until this point. "You gonna be good for your aunt, or we gonna have problems?"

The sight is enough to make my breath catch—the lethal biker holding my nephew like he's done it a thousand times before, the sheer size of him making Adam look impossibly small. And then Adam flashes a gummy smile, cooing up at Hawk as if the man just hung the moon.

My ovaries practically detonate.

Uh-oh.

Desperate for a distraction from the sudden warmth pooling low in my belly, I focus on the bottle, pouring the warmed milk with more care than necessary.

"How did you know I'm their aunt?" My voice comes out shakier than I'd like, but I don't dare meet his gaze, not when I can still feel the ghost of his touch lingering on my skin.

"Duck."

I nod, shaking the bottle to disperse the milk, then test it against my skin.

"Okay, we're good." I hold out my arms for Adam. "Thanks for the use of your microwave. We'll just be going—"

Hawk plucks the bottle from my hand, offering it to Adam with an ease that surprises me. Adam takes it, greedily pulling at the nipple.

"Boy's got an appetite," Hawk says with a chuckle.

He may be a bit of a jerk, but the sight of this big, bad, scary biker feeding my baby nephew does strange and wonderful things to my libido.

I am not attracted to Hawk. I am not attracted to Hawk. I am not attracted to Hawk.

"I'll take him now," I say, reaching for Adam.

Hawk shifts Adam to his shoulder, patting his back with surprising gentleness for such large hands. "I got him."

I open my mouth to argue, but honestly? Having someone else handle Adam for five minutes is too tempting to pass up.

Adam sucks down the milk like a champion, letting Hawk burp him with only the tiniest protest.

The traitor.

Hawk jerks his head toward the door. "Let's get him home."

"Bye, babe!" Ginger calls over her man's shoulder. "Don't be a stranger!"

I wave weakly, determined to never set foot in this place again.

The party has gotten rowdier in the short time we've been inside. More bikes line the street, their chrome glinting under the streetlights. Music still thumps, but the dancing has shifted from foreplay into all-out sex.

I hurry to keep up with Hawk's longer stride as we cross the street. Adam begins to make sleepy snuffle sounds, one tiny fist curling into the leather of Hawk's vest.

"Key?" Hawk asks when we reach Amanda's door.

I fish it from my pocket, very aware of his large presence behind me as I unlock the door. The house is dark and quiet—at least the twins are still sleeping.

"His room?" Hawk's voice is pitched low in the darkness.

"This way." I lead him down the hall, using my phone's flashlight to illuminate the path.

Hawk lays him down with the same careful movements he's shown earlier, his hands gentle as he settles Adam onto the mattress.

Something in my chest squeezes as I watch this big, dangerous man be so tender with my baby nephew.

"Thanks," I whisper. "For everything. The microwave, bringing him home..."

Hawk straightens, turning to face me. The shadows sharpen the cut of his jaw. The dim glow of my phone screen flickers between us, painting him in half-light, half-shadow, making it impossible to read his expression. But the heat rolling off him? That's unmistakable.

He takes a step closer.

Then another.

I retreat instinctively, my back pressing into the hard edge of the dresser, pulse skittering faster. His presence is overwhelming—too much, too close—but I can't seem to stop him. Can't make myself want to.

His hands rise, bracketing me on either side, palms flat against the wood. The scent of leather and motor oil surrounds me, and for a breathless second, all I can do is stare up at him, chest tight with something wild and unfamiliar.

"What are you doing?" I manage to ask. The words barely escape before he moves again—one hand sliding from the dresser to tangle in my ponytail.

"Warning you," he growls, then his mouth crashes down on mine.

His kiss is hard, demanding, stealing my breath and my sanity in equal measure. One of his hands holds me in place by my ponytail while the other trails up, fingertips grazing my throat. Not squeezing, just... holding. A show of strength. Control. His thumb presses lightly, tilting my head back, forcing me to open to him in this dark, intense, desperate kiss.

His tongue sweeps in, tasting, taking—possessing. His hand tightens just enough in my hair, holding me where he wants me as his grip at my throat reminds me exactly who's in control. He tastes of whiskey and something darker, more dangerous.

I should push him away. I have three kids sleeping under this roof. I have responsibilities, plans, a life I've carefully built that's already begun to disintegrate. My life is complicated enough without entanglements with dangerous men.

But oh, does it feel fucking good to be touched. Tasted. To be kissed with such reckless intensity.

My hands fist in his shirt, torn between pulling him closer and pushing him away. His body presses into mine, all hard muscle and blazing heat. One of his hands slides from my hip to tangle in my hair, tilting my head to deepen the kiss.

When his tongue sweeps into my mouth, electricity shoots through me, igniting every nerve ending. A whimper escapes before I can stop it.

God, how long has it been since I've been kissed like this? Have I *ever* been kissed like this? Like I'm being devoured, claimed, marked?

His other hand grips my hip, fingers digging in just shy of painful as he grinds against me. The dresser digs into my lower back, but I barely notice, too lost in the way he seems to be trying to crawl inside me through this kiss.

The rational part of my brain screams that this is a terrible idea. He's obviously involved in something illegal. I have the kids to think about. I can't afford indulgences.

But my body has other ideas, arching into his touch as heat pools low in my belly. Three days of stress, fear, and uncertainty melt away under the onslaught of sensation. For just a moment, I let myself get lost in it—in him.

He pulls back just enough to speak against my lips, his breath ragged. "If you don't want this, stay away from me. Because next time?" His teeth graze my bottom lip, sending shivers down my spine. "I won't stop."

And then he's gone. The loss of his heat feels like a physical shock. I grip the dresser to stay upright, my legs shaky and weak. My lips tingle where he kissed me, my body humming with unfulfilled need.

How am I supposed to stay away when every cell in my body is screaming for more?

"Well, fuck," I whisper into the darkness.

Things have just gotten that much more complicated.

5

HAWK

I've barely slept.

The taste of her is still on my lips—like honey and heat, like something I shouldn't have taken but couldn't resist. I've scrubbed my hands, brushed my damn teeth twice, but she's still there. Lingering.

Dawn breaks over the neighborhood as I step onto the front porch, the sun crawling slow over the horizon to stain the sky with soft golds and blues. My coffee is piping hot but not enough to clear my head. The aftermath of last night's party sprawls across the lawn—empty bottles, passed-out bodies, the stale scent of weed and spilled booze hanging thick in the air. The kind of mess I should be dealing with.

But all I can think about is her.

Brandi. Andi with an i.

I told myself I went over there to keep things clean. To warn her. Scare her a little. Make sure she understood who she was dealing with—who *I* was. A sergeant-at-arms doesn't leave loose ends. And she'd been on the verge of unraveling, already too close to shit she didn't need to be mixed up in.

That was the plan.

So why the hell can't I stop thinking about the way she trembled when I got close? The way her breath hitched when I touched her? How her lips parted just enough, like she was daring me to take, to taste?

I didn't go there to kiss her.

Hell, I hadn't even let myself consider it. But when she'd stood there, staring up at me with those wide, defiant eyes, lips pink and parted, it was like something inside me *snapped.*

One kiss.

That's all it was supposed to be—one taste, enough to break whatever spell she'd woven over me since the moment she stumbled into my life. But it hadn't been enough. Not even close.

I tossed and turned all night, restless, burning. Thinking about the way she felt against me—soft, curvy, her body fitting mine like she was made for it. About the feel of her tongue against mine, the desperate little sound she made when I gripped her ponytail and tilted her head back.

And I wanted *more.*

It wasn't just the kiss—it was *her*. The way she looked up at me, fierce and vulnerable all at once. How she didn't flinch when I crowded her. How she met my stare like she wasn't afraid of what she saw in me.

Plenty of women made offers last night—slipping hands under my cut, brushing close with sultry looks, whispered promises. Easy, meaningless relief. And I didn't give a damn.

Because none of them were *her*.

Andi's under my skin now, tangled up in ways I can't seem to shake loose.

Fuck.

I round the corner of the porch to the sitting area and Ginger's curled up on one of the deck chairs, Tank's jacket draped over her like a blanket. She stirs when I walk past.

"Coffee?" she asks hopefully, brushing away stray hairs.

"Kitchen."

She stretches, Tank's jacket sliding to the ground. "You seem grumpier than usual."

I grunt, scanning the street. The house across the road is quiet, dark.

Is she up yet? Are the kids?

Stupid to wonder. Stupider still to care.

"That new neighbor," Ginger says, a smile playing at her lips. "She seemed nice."

"Don't."

"Don't what? I'm just saying, the way you handled that baby..." She wiggles her eyebrows.

I shoot her a look that would have prospects pissing themselves. Ginger just laughs.

"Coffee," I remind her, hoping she'll take the hint.

She gets up, stretching again. "You know, some of us remember what you were like with your sister's kids, before—"

"Ginger." My tone carries a warning even she won't ignore.

She holds up her hands in surrender and heads inside, leaving me with memories I'd rather forget and the ghost of a kiss I can't shake.

The clubhouse slowly comes to life around me. Prospects stumble to clean up, nursing hangovers as they collect bottles and trash. Tank emerges from somewhere inside, looking rough but giving off the air of a guy well satisfied.

Ginger must have found him.

Duck's truck pulls up around eight. He looks fresh, probably thanks to his old lady kicking him out early. He takes one look at my face and chuckles.

"Rough night?"

I just stare at him.

"Right." He claps a hand on my shoulder. "The boys are following. I'll get more coffee on."

The rumble of bikes draws my attention to the street. Lee pulls up first, his father close behind. Stone might be president, but his son has inherited his commanding presence. At thirty, Lee is already making a name for himself as our enforcer, though most of us still remember him as the awkward teenager who grew up in the club.

"Rough night?" Lee calls out, killing his engine. He pulls off his helmet, revealing the face that has half the women in town trying to reform him. Dark hair, cut military short, sharp cheekbones, and our president's steel-gray eyes. The slash of a scar through his left eyebrow only adds to the danger rolling off him, and he wears his *Enforcer* patch like he was born to it.

He nods toward the passed-out prospect on my lawn.

"Yours was rougher, from what I heard."

Lee flexes his right hand, knuckles bruised. "Fucker had a hard head."

I raise an eyebrow.

Stone hip-checks his son. "Lee took care of it. Not bad for a freshly minted member."

Stone moves like a man ten years younger, the only signs of age in the silver threading through his dark hair and beard. His weathered face tells stories of bar fights and hard years, but his eyes miss nothing. He might look like the kind of man you'd cross the street to avoid —all muscle and menace wrapped in leather—but those of us who know him have seen his strategic mind at work.

He knocked up his high school girlfriend at seventeen and then again at nineteen. He took over the club at twenty-five and turned us from a struggling chapter into a force. It takes a lot to be the main provider and carve your way through the club ranks to president. I can't help but admire the fucker.

"Coffee's inside. If you ask nicely, Duck might point you in the direction of some breakfast."

More bikes roll in while I stand on the porch, sipping coffee. Axel, our road captain, leads the pack. He kills his engine only to start barking orders at the barely conscious prospects sprawled across my lawn.

"Christ, Ax, let them nurse their hangovers first," Lee calls out, returning with a steaming mug. "Boys had a rough night."

Axel flips him off. "You baby them too much, kid."

"Not a kid anymore," Lee growls, but there's no heat in it. This is an old argument, worn smooth with repetition.

Duck returns, a frown on his wrinkled face. "Someone get a prospect to go check on Andi. Ginger said her power's out. She'll need someone to get ice for groceries if her fridge is fucked."

I kick myself for not thinking of that last night.

"I'll do it."

Lee's head snaps around. "Who's Andi?"

"The girl Hawk here was playing house with last night,"

Ginger sings out as she emerges from the kitchen with her coffee.

"Shut it," I warn, but the damage is done.

"Oh?" Stone's interest sharpens. "Didn't know you'd brought a girl around."

"I didn't." I cross my arms, glowering as these fuckers henpeck, practically delirious for gossip.

They're worse than a nursing home.

"She strolled in looking rumpled but cute as a button sometime after midnight," Ginger says, preening to her captive audience.

"It was after two, and she needed to use the microwave," I say flatly. "For the baby."

"Baby?" Axel asks, rejoining us now that the prospects are busy hauling ass. "Since when do we have babies at parties?"

"Since Hawk started adopting strays," Ginger smirks.

"You want to control your woman?" I ask Tank. He yawns, wrapping an arm around his harpy.

"Nope."

I sigh. "Don't we have bigger shit to worry about than my new mess of a neighbor?"

Stone's expression darkens. "Chapel. Ten minutes."

The others sober. This is business now.

Duck catches my eye as we head inside. "You know, if you're interested—"

"I'm not."

He raises his hands in surrender, but his knowing smile tells me he isn't buying it.

Neither am I.

The chapel sits off the back of the house, away from the chaos of the main living spaces. The heavy wooden table dominates the space, carved with the history of our club. Stone takes his place at the head, Tank to his right. The rest of us file in, taking our usual seats as prospects scramble to bring coffee and clear the empty bottles from last night.

Mack, our secretary, is already set up, his laptop open and reading glasses perched on his nose. He looks more like a biker than the business brains of our club, but the man has an encyclopedic memory. Beside him, Cash—our treasurer—is buried in paperwork, his brow scrunched into a frown as he hunches over figures.

For two young guys, they both take their jobs far too seriously.

"All right," Stone calls the meeting to order. "Mack, what's first?"

Mack adjusts his glasses. "Bike rally next month. We need to confirm numbers for security detail. Also got word from the Rattlers MC—they want to discuss expanding their run through our territory."

"'Discuss.' Is that what they're calling it these days?" Lee mutters.

"They've been peaceful lately," Axel points out. "Might be worth hearing them out."

"Numbers first," Stone directs. "Cash, what's our take from last quarter's runs?"

Cash shuffles his papers. "Up twenty percent from last year. Shop's doing well too, though we need more merch."

"Duck?" Stone asks.

"On it. I'm updating the patch design and will put the order in this week."

"You need anyone to take a second look at the design?"

If looks could kill, Cash would be six feet under.

"Do I need someone to look at a patch which *I* designed? The patch you're wearing right now? The patch I personally inked on most of you?" He scoffs. "The updates are minor so no, I don't fucking need a second *fucking* opinion."

Cash clears his throat. "Got it. Moving on, Duck's mechanic is bringing in restoration work from all over the state. She's really carving out a name for us in the territory."

My jaw clenches at the unexpected mention of Andi. For a woman I barely knew existed twenty-four hours ago, she's coming up a whole fuck of a lot.

I don't like it.

"Speaking of territory," I cut in, ready to move past the usual business. "We need to talk about Summit Development."

The room quiets. Stone leans forward, elbows on the table. "You've confirmed the rumors?"

I nod. "Three houses this week had utilities shut off—not including your girl's across the road last night." I nod at Duck.

"Well, fuck," Stone mutters, leaning back in his seat.

"It's not just utilities," I add, spreading out the notes I've been collecting. "Code violations appearing out of nowhere. Health and safety inspections. Noise complaints."

"They're manufacturing problems," Stone growls.

"Then swooping in to 'save' people with quick cash offers," I confirm. "But only on properties they want."

Mack pushes his glasses up his nose, frowning at my notes. "There's a pattern here."

"Yeah." I tap the map. "They're creating a corridor. Look —the Wilson place, the old factory, now these three houses. They're boxing in the elderly residents first."

"Easiest targets," Lee says, his voice hard.

Duck clears his throat. "Martha Wilson swore she'd never sell. Her daddy built that house."

"She said she'd accepted an offer last week. Amazing what foreclosure threats can do," I say. "Especially when you're on a fixed income and suddenly facing 'urgent' repairs from code violations."

"Fuckers," Tank mutters.

Stone studies the map, his expression thunderous. "We had a chat with some of the contractors who've been walking into town. Got one drunk last night. He said equipment's arriving next week for the factory lot. Once construction starts..."

"The surrounding houses become unlivable," Axel finishes. "Noise, dust, traffic—those old folks won't last a month."

"We need to slow them down," I say. "Create enough delays that they miss their permit deadlines."

"And protect our people," Lee adds. He looks at his father. "We've already lost one brother to these assholes, and we'll be damned if we let them drive out the folks who built this town."

Stone nods slowly. "Duck, how're those shell companies coming?"

"Paperwork's clean. We can start buying properties tomorrow, lease them back to the original owners at fair rates."

"Good." Stone's eyes meet mine. "Your neighbor—she notice anything about last night?"

I think of Andi, exhausted on her porch with three kids to feed and no power. "Not yet. But she might if we got guys coming and going at all hours."

"Keep an eye on her," Stone orders. "If we're right and Summit's targeting the street…"

He doesn't need to finish. We all know what happens to people who stand in Summit's way.

"I got it covered," I say, ignoring Duck's knowing look.

"Got some more intel from our new bestie Rico," Lee adds, stretching his long legs under the table. "Summit's got ties to the cartels. They're running money through their developments, cleaning it."

"Explains the pressure to build," Axel says. "Can't launder what isn't there."

"Any proof?" Stone asks his son.

"Nothing solid," Lee replies.

Stone nods, stroking his beard in thought. "We need to be smart about this. Summit's got reach. One wrong move…"

"What about the utility company?" Tank asks. "They've got to be in on it."

"My cousin works dispatch," Cash says, his voice like gravel. "Says all the shutoff orders are coming from up top, marked urgent."

"Follow the money," Mack mutters, making notes.

I think about Andi again, about those kids. About all the other families Summit is targeting.

"We need more eyes on the ground," I say. "Regular patrols, especially at night. Document everything."

"Agreed." Stone looks around the table. "Lee, get your crew together. I want to know every move Summit makes. Duck, push that paperwork through—we need to start buying properties before they can."

"What about the construction site?" Axel asks.

A slow smile spreads across Stone's face. "Amazing how unreliable heavy equipment can be. All those mechanical problems..."

"Shame," Duck says with a shake of his head.

"Hawk." Stone's attention lands on me. "You need backup?"

I shake my head. "The prospects are enough for now. I'll let you know if that changes."

"Sounds good. Meeting adjourned," Stone announces. "Lee, Tank—stay back, I need a word. Rest of you, you know what to do."

I stand, my mind already racing with plans. Patrols to arrange, prospects to position, a neighbor to...

To what? Protect? Investigate? Seduce?

"Hawk." Duck's voice is low as we leave the chapel. "Andi? She's not just another complication. She's smart, she'll clue in if we're too obvious. But she's also vulnerable. If they're targeting this street, Summit might try to push her out to get the landlord to sell."

"I know."

"Do you?" He studies me.

"I'll handle it."

Duck sighs. "Fine. But try to leave her in one piece, if you can. It's hard to find decent employees these days."

I step aside, following him through the door, wondering what the hell I've done to deserve this.

6

ANDI

The knock comes just as I finish changing Adam's diaper.

"Coming!" I call, juggling the baby while trying to zip up my cutoffs. The power is still out, and the August heat is already making the house stuffy.

I open the door to find the barely dressed woman from last night—Ginger—standing on my porch. She's wearing tiny shorts and what appears to be a man's button-down shirt.

"Get dressed, honey," she says, beaming at me with far too much pep for this early in the morning. "You're coming with me."

I blink. "Excuse me?"

"Your power's out, the contents of your fridge are likely about to expire, and you've got three kids to feed." She peeks around me into the house. "Where are the twins?"

"Um, playing in their room, but how did you—"

"Perfect. Steel!" she calls over her shoulder. A mountain of a young guy appears at the bottom of my steps. "Get some prospects over here. We're moving her essentials to the clubhouse."

"We're *what*?" I squeak.

"Did I stutter?" She plucks Adam from my arms with practiced ease. "Duck filled me in. You need power, we have power. You need help, we have prospects who need something to do besides nurse their hangovers."

"I can't just—"

"You can and you will. Now, where's your go-bag?"

"My what?"

Ginger sighs dramatically. "Diaper bag? Baby stuff? Things required to keep tiny humans alive?"

"Second door on the right," I say, then shake my head. "Wait, no. I appreciate the offer but—"

"What are the twins' names?" she asks, breezing past me.

"Abby and Amy, but how do you know about—"

"Duck," she answers, still walking toward the hall. "Abby! Amy! Who wants waffles?"

Two squealing tornados shoot from their room, nearly taking Ginger out.

"Damn, that's fighting dirty," I mutter.

"Honey, I haven't even started fighting yet." She bounces Adam, who naturally snuggles right into her chest.

"He likes boobs," I grumble. "Any boobs, apparently."

"Smart boy." She turns toward Hawk's house. "Come on. I've got coffee and air conditioning."

"But—"

"And bacon."

My stomach growls traitorously.

"No, that's okay. We'll go out for breakfast and—"

Ginger cuts me off. "Babe. Stop. You've had a rough few days having this thrust upon you. Let us help."

I hate how my resolve weakens. "Just breakfast."

Her grin nearly blinds me. "We'll see. Come, girls!"

Twenty minutes later, I'm standing in the clubhouse kitchen, eating waffles while I watch a parade of leather-clad men carry my kids' essential belongings across the street. The twins, having inhaled their food, are in the front yard with Steel, climbing all over the prospect as he ignores their delighted shrieks.

"Put that in the front spare room," Ginger directs a young prospect struggling with Adam's cot. "And be careful with it!"

"I really don't think—" I start.

"Good. Don't think. Just drink your coffee and let us help." She shifts Adam to her hip. "Besides, Hawk won't mind."

"Hawk won't mind what?"

We both turn to find the man himself filling the doorway, his expression darkening as he takes in the scene.

"Perfect timing!" Ginger chirps. "Your new houseguests just arrived."

Hawk's gaze sweeps the kitchen, taking in the chaos—the half-eaten breakfast, the baby supplies scattered across the counter, Adam contentedly drooling on Ginger's shoulder.

"No," he says flatly.

"But they don't have power," Ginger explains, as if he's slow. "Or water."

"Not the MC's problem."

I set down my coffee. "Exactly what I said. Ginger, give me Adam, and we'll just be—"

"Actually," a gravelly voice interrupts. Duck appears behind Hawk, squeezing past him into the kitchen. "It *is* our problem. Club business."

Hawk's jaw ticks. "Duck."

"Hawk." Duck helps himself to coffee. "Ginger had a good idea."

"Ginger has shit ideas."

"Hey!" Ginger protests.

"The prospects need something to do," Duck continues

as if no one else is speaking. "And the clubhouse has the most space."

"There are hotels—" I start.

"Which cost money you need for other things," Duck cuts in. "Like diapers. And food. And lawyer fees."

I deflate. He isn't wrong.

"Besides," Duck adds with faux innocence, "having you here makes it easier to keep an eye on things. With all the... *problems*... in the neighborhood lately."

Something ugly crawls into my stomach. "Problems? What problems?"

Duck and Hawk exchange a look—one loaded with meaning I can't decipher.

"Fine," Hawk growls. "One night."

"A week," Duck counters.

"Two days."

"Five."

"Three," I interrupt. Both of them turn to me. "I'll call the utility company tomorrow and get this sorted. It'll probably take another day, maybe two, to turn it all back on."

"Deal," Duck agrees with a satisfied smile. "Welcome to the clubhouse, kid." He ruffles my hair then points a finger at the prospects who are hovering nearby. "No parties or public displays of affection until these kids are outta the house–you got me?"

Whatever answer the prospects may have offered is lost as Adam chooses right now to spit up all over Ginger's shoulder.

"That's my boy," I mutter, reaching for napkins. "Showing them exactly what they're getting into."

Ginger laughs, already heading for the sink. "Please. You think this is the worst bodily fluid that's been in this kitchen?"

"Or on your body, for that matter," Tank says, strolling into the kitchen. "Need a hand, babe?"

"I got it."

"And on that note," I say quickly, "I need to get the girls ready for—"

"Already done," Ginger sings out. "Steel's got them dressed and their teeth brushed."

I blink. "How did you—"

"I'm efficient." She winks. "And Steel's good at following orders. Speaking of..." She turns to Hawk. "Your room or the guest room?"

The muscle in Hawk's jaw jumps. "Guest."

"Shame." She grins. "Your room has so much more... space."

If looks could kill, Ginger would be a smoking crater in the floor.

I need to shut this down. Fast. "Listen, I appreciate everyone's help, but—"

A crash from the front yard interrupts me, followed by twin screams of delight.

"That's my cue," I sigh, heading for the door. But Hawk is already moving, his long stride eating up the distance.

"I got it," he growls.

I watch him go, trying—and failing—to ignore how his ass looks in those jeans.

"Don't fight it, honey," Ginger says softly beside me. "Sometimes you need to let people help."

"I don't need—"

"Yeah, you do. And that's okay." Ginger squeezes my shoulder. "Now come on, let's get you settled while the boys do the heavy lifting."

I let her lead me through the house, trying to convince myself this is temporary.

It's just for three days. What could possibly happen in three days?

Ginger gives me the full tour, starting at the entry and walking me through the clubhouse room by room.

The bones of the old farmhouse still linger, sturdy and proud, despite the renovations that have transformed it into something far more imposing. To the right of the entry is the garage, which backs onto the main bedroom. Down the hall and to the left are two bedrooms, a full bath, and another bedroom. It's in the front two bedrooms where the prospects place me and the kids. My bedroom is simple–a queen bed with a built-in closet and small desk. There's no room for a crib, so the kids are in the next door bedroom, their space slightly cramped with furniture but secure.

The original structure ended just past the hall. The main bedroom, now Hawk's, was once the heart of the home—the kitchen and dining area, if the old brickwork behind the bed is anything to go by. There's still a deep farmhouse sink built into one corner and it makes the space feel rooted. Lived-in. His personal space is massive, fitted with blackout curtains and a king-sized bed.

The final bedroom in the hall, now a guest room, was originally the lounge. The exposed beams in the ceiling and the scuffed hardwood floors are reminders of what it once was.

The ground floor was expanded when the previous owners blew out the back wall, creating a sprawling lounge and sitting area, expansive deck, and two additional rear bedrooms and bathrooms. The extension feels both modern and grounded, as if it was always meant to be there.

The leather furniture is worn but comfortable, and a massive sectional dominates the space, facing a large stone fireplace. Floor-to-ceiling windows let in the early morning light, while double doors open onto a back deck.

The kitchen and dining area have been pushed into the new extension, sleek and industrial with dark granite counters, a massive butcher block island, and steel appliances that gleam under the soft lighting. A long wooden farmhouse dining table, scarred and well-used, sits nearby, clearly built for feeding a crowd.

There's another hall at the rear of the dining room which leads through to yet another set of guest bedrooms neatly tucked away. These are cozy but simple, with a queen bed, a window overlooking the yard.

Up a set of gorgeous wooden stairs, the second floor feels entirely different. The modern renovation extends upward, designed for VIPs—visiting MC chapter presidents, allied clubs, or people the club's protecting. A great room with a second kitchen, a formal meeting room, and two large guest suites dominate the level. The guest suites have private sleeping areas, sitting rooms, and ensuites—comfortable, but still carrying that hard-edged, practical style. There's also a small meeting room, an office, two small bedrooms, another bath and a water closet. But its the library that holds my interest, surprising me with its well-stocked shelves heavy with both worn paperbacks and hardcovers. I could get lost up there for days if anyone would let me.

And then there's the attic. It's a fortress—there's no other word for it.

The space feels older and less touched despite the additions below it. But even here there are signs of the MC. A panic room hidden behind steel, a solid safe and spare armory built for protection.

"Just in case," Ginger says with a laugh as she shows me how to enter the panic room.

Beyond the house, the property sprawls across acres of land running the full length of the block. Trees ring the boundary, and yards of green grass, built up beds, and outbuildings dot the land.

The barracks, a converted barn, sits a short walk from the main farmhouse. It's rougher, less refined, and is where the prospects and lower-ranking members sleep. The scent of motor oil, sweat and sawdust lingers there. Practical. Crowded. Temporary.

The chapel, a smaller outbuilding, is off to the east, the windows double glazed and tinted.

"Don't go in there," Ginger warns as we stroll past. "That's for club members only."

The day rushes by in a chaotic shamble of moving furniture, cleaning out the fridge, and entertaining tiny humans. By the time I get them fed, bathed, and into bed, I'm utterly exhausted.

Closing the door gently on the kids' room, I tiptoe down the hall and out onto the back deck. The large yard is silent, the cool of the night having long since settled in.

The house feels different at night. Quieter, but with an undercurrent of tension that has nothing to do with the movie night happening in the garage.

I sit on the back deck, nursing a beer and listening to the baby monitor. The twins crashed hard after their exciting day of being spoiled rotten by bikers. Even Adam went down easily, probably worn out from being passed between Ginger and what feels like half the club's female population.

"They settle okay?"

I nearly jump out of my skin. For a big man, Hawk moves like a ghost.

"Jesus." I press a hand to my chest. "Make some noise next time."

He drops into the chair beside me, stretching out his long legs. "In my clubhouse, remember?"

Right. His club. His rules. His... everything.

"They're fine," I say, answering his original question. "Though I think Steel might have permanently damaged his reputation as a badass. Last I saw, the twins were trying to convince him to wear fairy wings."

A ghost of a smile crosses his face. "Prospects need to be broken in somehow."

We sit in silence for a while, the night air heavy with humidity and unspoken words. A loud cheer erupts from the garage, followed by laughter.

"You can join them, you know," I say. "You don't need to babysit me."

"It's fine." He props his booted feet up on the railing.

The night sounds swirl around us—a distant owl hooting in the trees, the rhythmic hum of cicadas, and the occasional rustle of leaves stirred by a faint, warm breeze.

The air feels thick with the scent of rain-soaked earth and the faint tang of gasoline drifting from the garage. Overhead, the moon hangs low, veiled by a patchwork of clouds that seem to trap the weight of the night, pressing down on us in a heavy, unyielding silence.

I pick at the label on my beer. "Look, about us staying. I appreciate the help, but—"

"But nothing. You're here until the power's back." His tone doesn't allow for argument.

More silence. More tension. More questions I'm not sure I want answered.

"The kids like you," I say finally, desperate to break the quiet.

"Kids are easy. They don't want anything from you except attention."

Unlike adults, goes unsaid.

"You have experience with kids?"

"Some." His voice flattens, warning me off that topic.

I take the hint, returning to my beer, but I feel his eyes on me, heavy as a touch.

"Why'd you kiss me?" The question slips out before I can stop it.

"Why'd you kiss me back?" he counters.

Touché.

I trace my finger through the condensation on my beer bottle. "That's not an answer."

"Neither is that."

The tension crackles between us, thick as the humid air. Another burst of laughter floats out from the garage, but it feels distant, removed from the bubble we've found ourselves in.

"This is a bad idea," I say finally.

"Probably."

"I have the kids to think about."

"I know."

"And you're obviously involved in something"—I wave my hand vaguely—"complicated."

His lips twitch. "That's one word for it."

"So we should just..." I trail off, not sure how to finish that sentence.

"Should just what?" He turns his head to look at me, moonlight catching the sharp angles of his face. "Pretend it didn't happen? Ignore it? Play house for three days and then what?"

"I don't know." The admission feels raw, honest. "I don't know anything anymore. Three days ago, my biggest worry was whether to replace my bike's spark plugs. Now I've got three kids, no power, and I'm sitting on a biker's porch trying to figure out why I can't stop thinking about that kiss."

"And?"

"And what?"

"Figure it out yet?"

I meet his gaze. "No. You?"

"Yeah." He shifts in his chair, his knee brushing mine. The contact is subtle but searing. "I figured out I want to do it again."

The baby monitor crackles with Adam's restless sounds before I can respond.

"I should—" I start to rise, but Hawk's hand comes down on my thigh, warm and unyielding.

"Give it a minute," he murmurs, voice like gravel. "He'll settle."

Sure enough, Adam's noises fade back to soft breathing.

Hawk's hand stays where it is. Heavy. Certain. Branding me through the worn denim of my cutoffs.

"This is still a bad idea," I whisper.

"Probably." The corner of his mouth curves, and his gaze locks with mine. Dark. Intense. Hungry. "But that doesn't mean we should stop."

And then his thumb moves.

He traces a slow, torturous circle against my bare skin just above my knee. Barely there, but the heat of it sinks deep, spreading like wildfire, coiling low in my belly until I can barely think past the sensation.

"I can think of plenty of reasons we shouldn't do this." But my protest sounds weak even to me.

"Name one." His voice drops lower, rougher. A challenge that seems to vibrate through my chest and dance across my skin.

"The kids."

"Sleeping."

"My job."

"Duck won't care."

I swallow hard. "You don't like me."

His thumb stills. "Who said that?"

The weight of that question hangs between us, heavy as the humid air. From the garage, another round of laughter drifts out, but it feels like it's coming from miles away.

I suck in a breath to answer—and then he leans closer.

The scent of him washes over me—whiskey, worn leather, and something distinctly *him*. Earthy. Masculine. It surrounds me, soothing and exhilarating at once, playing absolute havoc with my senses.

The tension in his face is carved deep—jaw tight, lips slightly parted like he's holding back. But it's his eyes that undo me. They *burrow* into mine, dark with hunger and something even deeper.

Possession.

My lips part, ready to speak—*beg* maybe—as his fingers dance higher, gliding along my thigh. Slow. Unrelenting. Until the calloused pad of his thumb brushes under the frayed hem of my shorts.

A breath catches in my throat, my body swaying toward him on instinct, desperate for more.

"Hawk—"

"You talk too much," he growls, voice ragged, and then his hand shifts, fingertips trailing higher, higher—until his thumb traces the sensitive skin of my inner thigh. Just enough to make my thighs tense. Just enough to leave me trembling.

"I—"

The baby monitor erupts with Adam's cry.

I jerk back, nearly falling out of my chair.

"Fuck," he grunts, his hand dropping away. "The timing on this kid."

I scramble. "I should—"

"Yeah," he mutters, already turning from me. "Run away, little lamb."

I hurry inside, my heart pounding against my ribs. Behind me, I hear the scrape of his chair, then the sound of his boots on the deck boards.

By the time I get Adam settled again, Hawk is gone, the only evidence he was there is the lingering warmth on my thigh where his hand had been and two empty beer bottles on the rail.

I touch my thigh, remembering the heat of his touch, the intensity in his eyes.

What the hell have I gotten myself into?

Somewhere in the distance, thunder rolls.

A storm is coming.

In more ways than one.

7

HAWK

"Hi."

The word drags me from unconsciousness. My hand is already moving toward the gun under my pillow before my brain registers the voice belongs to the tiny human standing beside my bed.

"Hi, hi!" another small voice pipes up.

I shift, finding another toddler on the opposite side of my bed.

Fuck.

I blink at the two tiny faces peering at me over the edge of the mattress. Abby and Amy—though damned if I can tell which is which—stand in matching pink pajamas, their dark curls wild from sleep.

"Why you here?" I growl, though I keep my voice low. No need to wake the whole house.

One of them announces something in garbled toddler-speak, patting my mattress with a chubby hand.

The other solemnly nods, seemingly in agreement.

I glance between them, confused when they stare at me expectantly.

"Um, okay?"

Squealing, they climb onto my bed, taking my unknowing invitation as gospel.

I glance at my phone. 6:15 AM. Jesus Christ.

"Your aunt know where you are?"

They both shake their heads, curls bouncing. The one not burrowing under my blankets lifts her arms in the universal "up" gesture.

I scrub a hand over my face. What the hell has my life become?

The blanket burrower manages to crawl onto the bed, examining my tattoos with sticky fingers.

"Pitty."

Her sister emerges from under the blanket, crawling closer to inspect the skull inked on my skin.

"Mmhmm," the bed burrower agrees.

Great. Not even seven AM, and I've got art critics.

"Hungy," the first one announces, patting my chest.

The other nods, vigorous and solemn. "Hungy, hungy!"

Christ. How does Andi do this every morning? Speaking of which…

"We should wake Andi," I suggest, hoping to redirect this toddler invasion.

Their little faces drop like I've kicked a puppy.

"Pahcake?" one asks, voice hopeful, eyes wide.

Her sister catches on fast. "Peeze?"

I'm the sergeant-at-arms of an MC. I've been in firefights, bar brawls, and more than one knife fight. I've broken bones, taken hits, and given worse.

But these two tiny humans, with their big eyes and hopeful faces?

They're going to be the death of me.

"Fine," I grumble. "But we're quiet, yeah? Let your aunt sleep?"

They nod solemnly… and immediately start giggling.

Cute—for a pair of runts.

Scooping them both up, I carry them through the house, trying to remember if the kitchen even has pancake mix.

"Weeee!" one squeals.

"Shh," her sister scolds.

At least one of them listens.

The kitchen is still dark, early morning light barely filtering through the windows. I deposit them both on the counter, keeping one hand on their backs so they don't topple off.

"Stay," I order.

They giggle again. Great. My intimidation tactics need work.

I open cupboards one-handed, searching for anything remotely breakfast-related. Beer, protein powder, more beer, some jerky... fuck. When's the last time anyone actually cooked?

"Whatcha doing?"

I turn to find Andi in the doorway, Adam on her hip. Her hair's a mess, her clothes are wrinkled from sleep, and there's a pillow crease on her cheek.

She looks sexy as fuck, and my dick takes fucking notice.

"Pahcakes!" the twins yell.

"Is that right?" She raises an eyebrow at me. "And did we ask Hawk if he wanted to make pancakes?"

Two tiny faces swivel to me, suddenly uncertain.

"Peeze?" they ask in unison.

Damn kids are going to own my ass at this rate.

"Don't know if I have any mix," I admit.

"You do," she says, adjusting Adam on her hip. "I grabbed

some yesterday when the prospects moved stuff from our place. Bottom cabinet by the fridge."

Sure enough, I spot grocery bags I hadn't noticed, filled with actual food.

"I figured they'd want pancakes since it's what they always demand at my place." She crosses to the coffee maker. "Though I didn't expect them to wake you up quite so early."

"Seeping," one twin says, pointing at her solemnly.

"So you decided to wake up Hawk instead?" She starts the coffee one-handed, like it's second nature.

They nod, all innocence.

"Rascals," she says, shaking her head before turning to me. "Sorry. They're usually good about staying in their room until—"

"It's fine." I pull out the pancake mix, frowning at the instructions. "Why does this have fifteen steps? How hard can pancakes be?"

Her laugh does something to me—something I don't want to think about.

"Oh honey," she says, still grinning. "Let me deal with Adam, and I'll help before you burn down the kitchen."

"I can handle it."

"Uh-huh." She smirks. "Just keep them from falling off the counter until I'm back."

I glance at the twins, who are now reaching for the sink.

"Stay," I growl again.

They giggle.

Definitely need to work on my intimidation tactics.

"Choc-it?" one of them asks hopefully.

"No chocolate," I say firmly.

Both their little faces drop.

"Choc-it," the other says sadly.

"I don't have any—"

"Second shelf, behind the coffee mugs," Andi calls from the hallway. "I bought chocolate chips too."

The twins perk up immediately.

"Traitor," I mutter, but I'm already grabbing the chocolate chips.

"Yay!" they squeal, bouncing on the counter.

"Hey, what did I say about staying still?"

They freeze mid-bounce, grins wide and completely unrepentant.

The rumble of bikes pulling up draws my attention out the window. Lee and a few prospects are here early for the morning meeting. They'll be reporting in after last night's reconnaissance.

Great. Just what I need—witnesses to my domestication.

"Brrroom, brrroom!" one of the twins exclaims, catching sight of the bikes.

"No," I say quickly. "We're staying here and making pan—"

"Steel!" they shriek, spotting the prospect walking past the window.

Steel freezes like a deer in headlights. The look on his face would be funny if I wasn't wearing the same damn expression.

"Well," Andi says, returning sans baby, "looks like we're having company for breakfast."

The twins beam.

I'm so fucked.

"Yo, brother," Lee calls, walking in through the side door. "We're early but—" He stops short, taking in the scene: me, two toddlers, and a bowl of pancake mix. "Well, shit."

"Morning," I growl.

"More pahcakes!" one of the twins demands.

"Peeze," the other adds, all charm.

Lee's grin spreads slow and wide. "Are you... making pancakes?"

"Shut it."

"Choc-it!" one twin announces proudly, like that explains everything.

Andi moves around me to grab a bowl, her arm brushing mine. "Lee, right? Coffee's nearly ready if you want some."

"Babe, I wouldn't miss this show for anything." Lee drops into a kitchen chair. "Steel! Get in here! You gotta see this."

The prospect hesitates in the doorway until the twins spot him.

"Up!" they demand in unison.

Steel looks at me like I might shoot him for touching the kids.

Smart kid.

"They're not going to bite," Andi says, pouring juice. "Much."

"They already like you," I add. "Might as well accept your fate."

Steel shuffles over, immediately getting grabbed by tiny hands.

"Fairy!" one of the twins declares.

"No fairy," Steel protests weakly.

"Yes fairy," the other insists.

Lee's laughter fills the kitchen. "Oh man, wait till the others hear about this."

I point my spatula at him. "One word and I'll tell Stone about Kya."

His laughter dies instantly. "You wouldn't."

"Try me."

"Who's Kya?" Andi asks, hip-checking me out of the way. "And you're doing that wrong. Here, let me."

"No one," Lee mutters, glaring at me.

The twins have already moved on to braiding Steel's hair–or at least twisting it up in knots.

Just another morning in the MC.

An hour later, the kitchen's a war zone of sticky plates and scattered chocolate chips. The prospects have filtered in one by one, drawn by the smell of food and the sound of laughter.

Now they're all sprawled around the kitchen in various states of food coma while the twins nap on Steel's chest, where he's passed out on the couch.

"Church in ten," Duck calls, poking his head in.

I nod, my gaze catching on Andi as she wipes down the counter one-handed, Adam balanced easily on her hip. She moves through the club's kitchen like she belongs with us, humming softly under her breath as she works.

Jesus. I need her either gone or under me before this attraction burns me alive. No woman has ever managed to get under my skin like Andi with an i.

"I got this," she says, catching my look. "Go do your mysterious biker business."

Her tone's light, but her sharp gaze misses nothing—not the looks between me and Duck, not the way conversations stop when she walks in, not the careful way we all talk around certain subjects.

"You sure?"

I mentally kick myself for the question. The woman is perfectly capable of looking after herself, but I can't help but ask.

She raises an eyebrow. "I think I can handle cleanup and three sleeping kids. Besides"—she nods toward Steel —"looks like I've got help."

Poor bastard doesn't stand a chance.

"Alright, boys," I call out. "Let's move."

The prospects scramble to their feet, trying to look alert despite their pancake-induced comas. Lee stretches lazily, shooting Andi a wink that makes my hands itch to knock him out.

"Thanks for breakfast, darlin'."

"Any time," she replies easily. Too easily.

I watch her for another beat before I turn, heading out of the kitchen.

Time to focus. We've got a development company to deal with. I don't have time to think about how the woman in my kitchen tastes.

Chapel's already full when I walk in. Stone stands at the

head of the table, maps spread out in front of him. The room quiets as I take my seat.

"Nice of you to join us," Stone says dryly. "Heard you were playing house."

There's snickering around the table. I shoot Lee a look promising retribution.

"Got news," I say, ignoring the jabs. "Erica Olsen came by last night after everyone cleared out."

That sobered them up.

"And?" Stone leaned forward.

"Summit's pushing hard. Sent some guys around yesterday afternoon. Said there'd been complaints about her yard. Code violations." I pulled out the notice she'd shown me. "Giving her forty-eight hours to clean it up or they're fining her ten grand."

"Bullshit," Duck growled. "Her yard's perfect. She's got fucking prize-winning roses."

"Exactly." I spread out the paperwork. "Notice came from the city, but look at the letterhead."

Mack adjusted his glasses, studying it. "This isn't the usual department."

"Because it's not real," Lee said. "They're manufacturing violations now?"

"Getting bolder," Stone muttered. "What else?"

I grit my teeth. "Erica mentioned that three more houses in her street got notices this past week. All elderly residents. All prime locations for Summit's development plans."

"They're closing in," Axel said. "Creating a corridor just like you said."

Stone studies the map, his expression thunderous. "Lee?"

Lee leans forward. "Prospects and I made it into the construction office without any issues." He pulls a sheet of paper from his pocket and tosses it on the table. "There's your list. Fuckers aren't even hiding it."

The printout has a list of houses across town they're targeting.

"Fuck." Stone shakes his head. "Alright, tomorrow's Monday. We start. Duck, offer Martha Wilson whatever she wants plus the opportunity to stay in her home for the rest of her life. Same for the others." Stone looks around the table, his gaze landing on Axel. "Axel, volunteer the prospects. Put the word out. Anyone in the area who gets a fucking fine or notice can call on us to help them with repairs, clearing, whatever they need."

Axel nods solemnly.

Stone meets each of our eyes individually. "Anyone got a problem putting their cut toward this?"

Head shakes all around.

"Good." He turns to Lee. "Your crew ready?"

Lee's grin is all teeth. "Just say when."

"Tonight. I want those construction vehicles disabled before they can break ground."

"What about the utility company?" Tank asks.

"Working on it," Cash says. "My cousin's looking into it."

"Perfect." Stone glances around again. "Alright. Let's get to work."

8

HAWK

The clubhouse is dark when I get home except for a soft glow from the kitchen. It's after midnight, and I'm not expecting to find anyone up and moving. Instead, I find Andi in the kitchen, Adam cradled in one arm as she feeds him. She glances up as I enter, her eyes widening slightly at my, no doubt, disheveled look.

Let's just say tampering with construction vehicles isn't exactly the easiest—or cleanest—job.

"You look like shit," she says softly, mindful of the other occupants in the house.

"Feel like it." I drop into a kitchen chair, exhaustion hitting hard now that I'm home. The smell of something delicious lingers in the air, tempting my tastebuds. "You cooked?"

"Lasagna. I made you a plate. It's in the fridge, if you're hungry."

"Fuck yes."

She begins to move but I wave her off.

"Stay. I can get it." I push myself up, ignoring the protests of bruised muscles. "You've got your hands full."

She smiles, leaning back as Adam quietly sucks at the remainder of his formula.

I grab the plate, watching her as I reheat my food. She's beautiful like this—soft and unguarded in the middle of the night, humming quietly to the baby as he eats. Her hair is loose around her shoulders, and she wears an old T-shirt over faded sleep shorts. The sight does something to my insides.

This is a side of her the garage never sees. The ice queen mechanic, melted into this gentle creature who stays up late to feed a baby that isn't even hers.

"He always eat this late?" I ask, sitting down with my plate.

"Mm. Like clockwork."

I raise an eyebrow. "My sister has kids. I don't remember them needing multiple feeds at his age."

She lifts one shoulder in a half-shrug. "He was born early. He's small for his age. The doctor said the extra feeds aren't a bad thing at this point. She suggested he'll grow out of it when he's ready."

I nod, lifting my fork to stab a mouthful of the piping hot lasagna.

"Wasn't expecting you to cook." The words come out rougher than intended. "Thanks."

Her eyes meet mine. "You're welcome." A small smile curves her lips. "It's the least I can do when you're putting up with us."

I lift my fork to my mouth, wincing as my body protests. The cuts have started bleeding again, and I'm pretty sure the shoulder is bruised.

Fucking hell.

"Jesus, Hawk." She leans across the table to catch my hand, examining the damage. "What did you do, punch concrete?"

Close enough. Summit's equipment had been a little more stubborn than expected.

"It's nothing."

She shoots me a look that says she isn't buying it. "Stay put. Let me put him down and grab the first-aid kit."

I watch as she disappears down the hall, the baby now milk-drunk and sleepy against her shoulder. Her quiet efficiency with him, the natural way she soothes his fussy noises, it hits me right in the chest.

What the fuck? When did I start finding maternal instincts so damn sexy?

She returns minutes later with a battered first-aid kit.

"You don't have to—"

"Shut up and eat." She pulls her chair closer, taking my free hand. "If I don't clean this it'll get infected."

Her touch is gentle, but her mouth is set in that stubborn line I'm coming to know well. This isn't a battle I'll win.

I hide a smile. "Yes, ma'am."

She works saline across the cuts, gently cleaning out the dirt and grit before applying ointment and bandages. I eat quietly while she attends to one hand, then swap over my fork to my left, allowing her to tend to the other.

"You're good at this," I say, watching her methodical care of my hands.

"Lots of practice." She dabs antiseptic on my knuckles with a gentleness that belies her usual tough exterior. "Though my usual patients are accident-prone twins."

Her gaze meets mine. "I guess I better add bikers who can't seem to avoid trouble to that list."

"Wasn't looking for trouble. But it's my job to finish it when it arrives."

"What do you mean?"

"It's part of my role in the club." At her raised eyebrow, I tap my patch. "As sergeant-at-arms, I'm in charge of keeping order and making sure we're safe."

"So you're essentially security? Or like a police officer?" she asks.

"Something like that. Basically what it means is

sometimes I need to yell at people, and sometimes I come home with bloody knuckles."

"And tonight?" She secures the bandage with tape. "The yelling didn't work?"

"Not so much." I flex my fingers, testing her handiwork.

She's quiet for a moment, her thumb absently brushing over my knuckles. "Does it bother you? The violence?"

The question catches me off guard. There's no judgment in her voice, just genuine curiosity.

"No," I say honestly. "Not when it's necessary. Not when it protects what matters."

Her eyes lift to mine. "And what matters?"

"The club. Family." I catch her hand before she can pull away. "People worth protecting."

Something flickers in her expression—understanding maybe, or recognition. She knows what it means to protect what's yours. I've seen her with the kids, fierce and protective as any mama bear.

She brushes her thumb over the corner of the bandage. "This one might scar."

"I'll add it to the collection."

Her thumb traces an old scar on my forearm. "Got stories for all of these?"

"Some better than others." I turn my arm, letting her fingers trail over the marked skin. "Though most aren't suitable for polite company."

"Good thing I'm not polite company then."

The teasing note in her voice does things to me. "No," I agree. "You're something else entirely."

Our gazes hold for a beat too long before she glances away, clearing her throat. "Well, you're all done."

I tighten my grip on her fingers before she can pull away completely. "Thank you."

She shrugs. "It's just some bandages."

"Not to me." My voice comes out rougher than intended. "Been a long time since anyone's cared enough to patch me up."

Something soft flickers in her expression before she ducks her head. "Well, don't get used to it. The next time you come limping in after midnight, I'll hopefully be fast asleep."

"Speaking of, you should head to bed," I say finally, noting the shadows under her eyes.

"Probably." But she makes no move to leave. "You okay? Really?"

The concern in her voice undoes me. "Yeah. Better now." I tap a finger against the now empty plate. "This was great. Thanks." She stands, gathering my plate. "Any time. Though maybe next time try to make it home before the food gets cold."

"Yes, ma'am."

Her free hand brushes my shoulder, the touch brief but warm. "Get some sleep, Hawk. Those knuckles need rest."

I watch her move to the sink, the quiet domesticity of her rinsing the plate hitting me right in the chest. She fits here, in my clubhouse, in my kitchen, in my space.

I stay up, nursing a beer long after she's retired. The ghost of her touch lingers on my skin.

Andi is a dangerous woman.

I find I like it.

9

ANDI

"What do you mean you won't accept payment over the phone?"

I pace Duck's office, phone pressed to my ear, trying not to curse out the utility company's fourth representative.

Ginger had arrived that morning with Steel in tow.

"You need to work and I have a free day," she said, bundling up the kids and hustling me out of the house with a cheerful wave. "Go! We'll be fine."

I don't know what it says about me that I left babysitting duties to a woman I barely know and a biker prospect. But I need the cash.

"I'm sorry, ma'am, but for this account, we can only accept payment by check."

I stifle a scream. I've been fighting with the utility company for over an hour, pacing back and forth in

Duck's tiny office at the garage as I've been passed through person after person who doesn't seem able to help me.

"That makes no sense. You're really telling me you won't accept my cash, and I have to wait until you get a fucking check in the mail before you'll turn my shit back on?"

"Language, ma'am. And yes. The account status has been changed. We can only accept checks or in-person cash payment for this account."

Through the window, I see Duck and Hawk talking by a restored Harley. They've been hovering all morning, taking turns finding reasons to walk past the office.

Normally I'm out the back of the garage, elbow deep in engine. I rarely see the customers during the day—and if I do, it's normally because I have to be the one to tell them the bad news.

"Changed by who? Why?"

"I don't have that information, ma'am. If you'd like to mail a check—"

"It'll take five days to process! I have three kids in that house."

"I understand your frustration, but—"

"No, you don't. Because if you did, you'd take my damn payment." I grip the phone tighter. "Let me speak to your supervisor."

"They'll tell you the same thing. Check or cash only."

"Fine. Where's the closest office front?"

"One moment, let me check."

He takes his time, coming back five minutes later. "Lexington Gardens."

I cough. "Are you shitting me?"

"Ma'am, language!"

"Dude, Lexington Gardens is five hours' drive away. You're telling me you have nothing closer?"

"That's correct."

"Fine," I snap. "Give me the mailing address."

The representative rattles off an address, and I scribble it down.

"Okay, how long will this take to process?"

"Five days for the check, then we'll send someone out in five to ten business days."

"Dude, come on. This is a joke. I have three kids to take care of."

"Then you should have paid your bills on time."

I bite back the curse on the tip of my tongue. Yeah, Amanda really should have paid her bills. Now I'm out nearly five grand in overdue notices and potentially homeless until these guys get their act together.

"Is there anything else?" the guy asks, his voice dripping with smugness.

"No," I grind out through gritted teeth.

"You have a lovely day."

The line clicks dead, and I lose it. "Son of a bitch!"

"Problem?" Hawk's voice is carefully neutral.

I spin to find him and Duck watching me from the doorway. "They won't take my payment unless it's by check. Oh, or cash, but I have to drive to Lexington-fucking-Gardens to hand it over. Since when do utility companies refuse credit card payments?"

Duck and Hawk exchange a look I can't interpret.

"Sounds frustrating," Duck says mildly.

"Frustrating? It's—" I stop, sucking in a deep breath. "Sorry. I'm fine. I'll take this as a lunch break."

Duck tosses me a brown sack. "Then eat up. 'Cause we've got a fender-bender coming in that the guy wants a full repair on. '69 Mustang."

I wince. "His fault or the other guy?"

"His. Wanted to show off and put it through a fence."

I shake my head as I pull the sandwich from the bag. "Damn. People like that shouldn't own cars that precious."

"You're telling me." Duck jabs his elbow into Hawk's ribcage. "Go talk to the girl while I deal with this mess."

I freeze mid-bite. "Talk to me?" I ask around a mouthful of ham and tomato.

"I overheard." Hawk takes a seat, stretching out his long legs. "Sounds like you might need a place for a while longer."

I chew slowly, taking my time as I consider my options. "Look, it's not great," I admit. "It sounds like it'll be at least two, maybe three weeks. But don't worry. I'll figure something out."

My dwindling bank account says that "something" will need to be cheap. Maybe I can buy a tent and camp in the backyard.

"Hmm." Hawk makes a non-committal sound.

I take another bite, chewing even slower as my brain races.

Maybe there's a cheap motel around somewhere. But where would I take the kids during the day? There's nothing close by. I could move them back to my apartment, but I have to be out of my place by next week, and I already organized movers to store my stuff until I can find us a better place.

Which leaves me screwed. I'd still have to figure out somewhere to live unless I want to sign a twelve-month lease on a one-bedroom apartment.

Not happening.

Panic starts to claw its way up my throat as I feel the walls of my carefully constructed life crumble around me.

I set the sandwich back down with shaking hands, my

stomach clenching with panic. My mouth tastes like sawdust and I swallow, drying to draw moisture in.

This isn't good. We're going to be homeless. We'll have to live in a borrowed car. CPS will take them. I'll be branded and unfit—

"Stay." Hawk's voice cuts through my spiraling thoughts.

I jerk upright. "What?"

"Stay. At the clubhouse. Until this gets sorted."

"I can't—"

"You can and you will." His tone leaves no room for argument. "The kids are settled. Steel's apparently been promoted to personal fairy. And Ginger's..." He pauses. "...well, Ginger's Ginger."

"That's what worries me," I mutter. I left the twins braiding Steel's hair while Ginger supervised, baby Adam happily drooling on her shoulder. She's a great person and it would be far too easy to become reliant on her for support.

I knew better than to look to others for help—no matter how nice they seemed.

"Look," Hawk leans forward, his elbows on his knees. "Something's not right with this situation."

"You think?" I ask, rolling my eyes.

His expression darkens. "Fuck it. You're not the only one impacted by this."

My eyebrows rise. "What do you mean?"

He hesitates. "Let's just say you're not the first person to experience this bullshit."

I wait, frowning when he doesn't continue. "You want to elaborate?"

"No."

I crumple the wrapper from my sandwich. "Right. Mysterious biker business."

"Andi—"

"It's fine." I stand, brushing crumbs from my coveralls, my appetite gone. "I appreciate the offer to stay, but—"

"But nothing." He rises too, crowding my space. "You're staying. End of discussion."

"You can't just—"

"I can and I am." His eyes hold mine. "Unless you want to explain to those kids why they have to leave a home for— what are you thinking? A motel? A tent?"

Low blow. And far too close to the truth.

It rankles that he has something over me.

"Two weeks," I concede. "Max." I poke him in the chest. "And no biker business. You keep that shit to yourself. Got me?"

His shoulders relax, but his eyes darken as he catches my finger, holding it against his chest. "Careful, little lamb.

Keep touching me like that, and I might forget why this is a bad idea."

My breath catches. "Which part?"

"You. Under the same roof." His thumb traces circles on my wrist. "In my space. Smelling like my soap."

"I—"

"Making pancakes in the morning." He steps closer, still holding my wrist. "Walking around in those tiny shorts after the kids are asleep. Anyone ever tell you that your thighs make a man think of sex?"

Considering I'm a size eighteen on a good day—the answer is no.

Not that I'll ever tell him.

Heat blooms on my cheeks. "Hawk—"

"You want to know why I'm doing this?" His other hand comes up, and I flinch away.

"What are you doing?"

"You have some grease." He gently cups my cheek, wiping the smudge from my skin.

"I'm doing this," he repeats, his gaze locked with mine, "because I can't decide if I want you gone or underneath me, and until I figure it out, I'm not letting you out of my sight."

I don't know how to take this admission. I open my mouth, searching for words, when a motorcycle roars into the parking lot. The sound is horrible and grinding—engine knocking, timing off.

"Damn it," I mutter, using the interruption to step back, my skin tingling where he touched me. "That better not be—"

"Andi," Duck calls from outside the office, tapping against the window. "He's fucked it this time."

I swear softly, stepping out from around Hawk. "I told that dick if he rode it before I checked the timing—"

The bike cuts off with an awful grinding sound.

"Yeah," Hawk drawls from behind me. "We're done here. Go fix his mess."

I shoot him a look over my shoulder. "This conversation isn't over."

"Yes, it is." His voice drops lower. "But we can start a different one later."

Heat pools in my belly at his tone, but I force myself to focus on the disaster pulling into the lot.

The Vincent Black Shadow is a classic—a British motorcycle produced from 1948 to 1955, the gorgeous import has a v-twin engine, cantilever rear suspension, and can reach a top speed of 150mph—not bad for an old bike.

They command high prices at auctions and are in high demand by collectors.

A pity its current owner is a guy with more money than the sense God gave a gnat.

"What did you do?" I demand as the rider dismounts.

"Nothing! It just started making this noise and—"

I hold up my hand. "Stop, Nicky. Just... stop talking before I cry."

Or punch you.

Behind me, I hear Hawk's low chuckle as he heads back to his bike.

"I'll pick you up at five," he calls over his shoulder.

"Why? I have a car," I remind him.

"Five, Andi. Be ready to ride."

"But the car. I need it for—"

He revs his bike, pulling out without waiting to listen.

I watch him go, torn between irritation and something warmer, more dangerous. He wants to take me for a ride. On his bike.

"You know," Duck says mildly beside me, "I've never seen him like this."

"Like what?"

"Invested."

I shake off Duck's words, reminding myself that I don't need another complication.

Turning back to the Vincent, I mutter, "Yeah, well, don't get used to it."

Duck's knowing chuckle follows me as I pop the bike's cover, ignoring Nicky's whining explanations while I check the damage the dickhead's inflicted this time.

Two weeks. I can handle two weeks.

Or so I tell myself.

ANDI

Motor oil is a bitch to get out from under your fingernails.

I scrub harder at the black crescents in Duck's tiny bathroom sink, wondering why I'm even bothering. It's not like Hawk hasn't seen me covered in grease earlier today. True, I'd become even more caked while wrestling with the Vincent's timing, but what's a little more filth between friends?

With a huff, I toss the scrubber into the sink and look up at my reflection in the mirror.

The woman staring back looks tired but strong—I'm broad shoulders and work-hardened muscles wrapped in abundant curves that never quite fit society's ideal. My dark auburn hair is pulled back in its usual messy ponytail, wisps escaping to frame a face that's more striking than pretty. Years of working on engines have left their mark in the tiny scars on my hands and the chipped nails.

I'm not small or delicate or any of the things men usually want. I learned early on that I'd never be anyone's idea of dainty. But my body is strong. Capable.

I love being me. I love my body, my life, my strength.

Even if sometimes, late at night, I wonder if anyone will ever see past the grease to the woman underneath.

God, why does this feel different? It's just a ride. Not like a... date. Right?

My phone buzzes on the sink edge. Ginger.

"You better be getting pretty," she sings when I answer.

"You know."

"I do," she laughs. "Now answer the question."

"I'm washing motor oil off my hands," I say, wedging the phone between my ear and shoulder. "How are the kids?"

"Perfect angels. Steel's already promised three tea parties, and Tank's been recruited as the dragon they need to slay."

A muffled protest in the background sounds suspiciously like a roar.

"Are you sure you don't mind—"

"Stop. The kids are fine. Tank is a big softie. He loves kids. Ours are all grown now, which makes me sad. They're smelly teens with their own lives, and I never got girls, only three boys who just want to make out with girls and guys and play ball. Ugh. Now, tell me you're not wearing those coveralls to this date."

"It's not a date."

"Babe. You're on the back of his bike. That's biker for *date*."

I glance at the bag I've stashed under the sink. "I had a change of clothes in my locker."

"Describe."

I sigh. "Jeans, a fluffy pink sweater, and a leather jacket."

"I mean... did you happen to grab makeup?"

"I have lip gloss."

"I'm hanging up now and coming right over."

"Ginger!"

Her laugh echoes through the phone. "Look, the guy is lost for you. Go have fun."

I mutter something under my breath.

"What was that, sugar?"

"I said I don't do fun."

"Hmm. When's the last time you did something just for you?"

I can't remember.

"It's just a ride," I say, turning back to the mirror. "You're turning it into something bigger than it is. He probably wants to talk about the house rules or something."

"Sure. Because bikers always take women on their bikes to 'talk' about rules. Unless we're talking bedroom rules, in which case—"

"Ginger!"

The rumble of a motorcycle pulling into the lot has my stomach doing flips.

"Well," Ginger practically purrs, "sounds like your chariot awaits."

I shake my head. "Good night, Ginger. Don't wait up."

She cackles as I hit end.

I toss the phone onto my bag and stare at my reflection. The woman looking back seems foreign—hair loose instead of tied back, a touch of mascara, lips glossed pink.

What the hell am I doing?

I change into the clothes, grab my bag, and head out, forcing myself not to overthink this.

Fat chance.

The sun is just starting to set, painting the garage lot in shades of gold and amber.

Hawk sits astride his bike, one boot planted on the ground. He's changed too—dark jeans, white T-shirt under his cut, his hair still damp like he's showered after whatever mysterious biker business he's been handling all day.

He looks dangerous. Devastating.

And he's watching me like I'm something he wants to devour.

"You clean up nice, little lamb," he says, his voice a low rumble that does things to my insides.

"You expected me to show up in coveralls?"

His eyes track down my body, lingering on the places where my jeans hug close. "Wouldn't have complained."

Heat blooms in my chest. "Right."

"But this..." He reaches out, catching a loose strand of my hair between his fingers. "This is something else."

"Good something?" The words slip out before I can stop them.

His eyes darken. "Very good." He holds out his spare helmet. "Ready?"

No. Not even close.

"Yeah," I say, taking the helmet. "I'm ready."

I hesitate with the helmet in my hands. "You going to tell me where we're going?"

"Get on and find out." His slow grin has my pulse jumping. "Trust me."

"About that..." I shift my weight, fighting the urge to run back inside. "Look, if this is about the house situation—"

"It's not."

"Then what is it about?"

He studies me for a long moment. "Maybe I just want to take a beautiful woman for a ride."

"Hawk—"

"And maybe," he continues, "I want to see if you taste as good as I remember."

Heat floods my cheeks. "That's... that's not fair."

"Never claimed to be fair." He pats the seat behind him. "Coming?"

I *should* say no. Should get in my car and drive home to the kids. Should do anything but climb onto a bike with a man who makes promises with his eyes that have my whole body humming.

Instead, I put on the helmet.

His answering grin is pure sin as I swing my leg over the bike, settling onto the seat behind him, keeping a safe, respectable distance. I know how to ride. I'm confident, capable. I've been on a bike plenty of times before—felt the power of the engine, the wind on my skin. But this?

Sitting *behind* Hawk is a whole new experience.

His presence makes the machine feel smaller, my whole world rapidly. My breathing is shallow, my pulse a frantic thrum I can't quite steady.

And then he moves.

His big hands slide under my thighs, the rough drag of his fingers against denim making my stomach flip. With a deliberate yank, he drags me forward, erasing the space I'd left between us. My leather-clad chest presses flush against the cold leather of his cut, my thighs snug against him. My nose grazes his neck, catching his scent—smoky leather, clean sweat, and something darker, *him*—intoxicating in the worst way.

Hawk reaches back, finds my hands, and reels me in tighter, wrapping my arms around his solid middle until there's no space left between us. Until my body molds to his, every hard line of him pressing into every softer curve of me.

No words. No teasing.

He just *holds* me there. Firm. Possessive. Unrelenting.

And when he finally speaks, it's a growl that rumbles right through my chest, setting every nerve on fire.

"Hold on tight."

The bike roars to life between my thighs, but it's nothing compared to the storm he's unleashed inside me.

The late spring air whips past as we wind through town, the familiar streets looking different from the back of Hawk's bike. My thighs press against his, my chest molds to his back, and each curve in the road has me holding tighter.

We head up toward the mountain, taking the twisting road that overlooks the valley. The sun sets behind us, casting long shadows across the pavement.

I've ridden this road a hundred times on my own bike, but this is different. Every vibration, every lean into a turn, sends heat pooling low in my belly. And from the way Hawk's hand occasionally squeezes my knee when we stop, he knows exactly what this ride is doing to me.

He pulls over at the overlook, killing the engine. The sudden silence feels heavy, charged.

"You can let go now," he says, amusement coloring his voice.

I realize I'm still pressed against him, my fingers curled into his shirt under his cut.

"Right." I unclench my hands, sliding off the bike on shaky legs.

The view takes my breath away—the whole town spread out below us, lights starting to twinkle on as dusk settles. Up here, everything looks peaceful, perfect.

"Beautiful, isn't it?"

I turn to find Hawk watching me instead of the view, his eyes dark with intent.

"Yeah," I manage. "It is."

He moves closer, reaching up to help with my helmet. His fingers brush my neck as he unsnaps the strap, and I can't quite suppress my shiver.

"Cold?" he asks, though his smirk says he knows better.

"No."

"Good." His hand lingers at my neck. "Hungry?" he asks, though his eyes say he isn't talking about food.

"Shouldn't you have asked that before bringing me up a mountain?"

His laugh is low, rich. "I know a place. Good view. Better food."

"As long as it's not a biker bar," I say, thinking of the chaos at his house. "I've seen enough half-naked women for one week."

"Jealous?"

"No. I'm impressed. I could never."

He steps closer, his fingers trailing from my neck to my collarbone. "Really? Cause I think you'd look great half-naked."

My breath catches as his thumb traces circles on my skin. "Hawk—"

"I like how you say my name." His other hand settles on my hip. "Like you're not sure if you're warning me off or asking for more."

Heat blooms everywhere he touches.

"Which is it?" He dips his head, his lips brushing my ear. "Tell me what you want, little lamb."

The nickname should annoy me. Instead, it sends shivers down my spine.

"Food," I manage. "You promised food."

He pulls back just enough to meet my eyes, his expression promising all sorts of things that have nothing to do with dinner. "Food first."

"First?"

His grin is pure sin. "Then we see if you taste as good as I remember."

I swallow hard. "That's... that's not playing fair."

"Never claimed to be fair." He steps back, holding out his hand. "Coming?"

This is such a bad idea. But as I put my hand in his, I can't bring myself to care.

The restaurant sits nestled into the mountainside, windows overlooking the valley below. String lights twinkle along the rustic wooden deck, and the smell of grilled food makes my stomach growl.

"Not what you expected?" Hawk asks, helping me off the bike.

"I figured we'd end up at some dive bar with peanut shells on the floor."

"That's tomorrow night."

"Funny."

His hand settles on my lower back as he guides me inside. The hostess's eyes widen slightly at Hawk's cut; this seems like the kind of place you'd normally need to wear a tie for, but she just plasters a smile on her face and leads us to a corner table with a view.

"This is…" I look around at the intimate lighting, the couples sharing wine and quiet conversation. "Nice."

"Don't sound so surprised." He pulls out my chair. "I do know how to treat a woman."

"Apparently."

His eyes darken. "You haven't seen anything yet."

The wine is good, the food even better. Conversation flows easily—he asks about my work, and we bond over motorcycle wreck horror stories. I tell him stories about the twins and Adam; he tells me about his time serving overseas.

We carefully avoid talking about the club or my situation with Amanda.

It feels… normal. Almost too normal.

"You're thinking too hard," he says as we finish our meal.

"Just wondering when the other shoe's going to drop."

"Why does it have to?"

I trace the rim of my wine glass. "Because good things don't just happen. Not in my experience."

"Maybe it's time for some new experiences."

The heat in his voice has me meeting his eyes. The way he's looking at me… like I'm something he wants to devour.

"What do you do for a job?" I ask, suddenly curious that he hasn't disclosed.

He leans back in his chair. "I own Stoneheart Security."

I frown, trying to work out how I know the name. "Oh, that's the company that handles security for Duck, right?"

He nods. "We do a bit of everything. Businesses, private contracts, security systems, some bodyguard work." His lips quirk. "We even do the odd celebrity."

"Huh." I try to reconcile this new information with what I know of him. "So you're like... a legitimate businessman?"

His laugh is low and rich. "Don't sound so shocked."

"I'm not shocked, I just..." I gesture vaguely at his cut. "Didn't expect that. Not in this small town, anyway."

"What did you expect?"

"I don't know. Professional badass? Lady-killer? Definitely not someone who worries about thieves in the night."

He snorts. "Don't underestimate football nights. Those drunk dads get pretty rowdy on their way home."

I laugh, surprised by his dry humor. "So that's how you afford your ride."

"Among other things." His phone buzzes, and he glances at it briefly before turning it face down. "Ready to get out of here?"

My pulse jumps at his tone. "And go where?"

His smile is wicked. "Anywhere you want, little lamb."

"Want to take the long way home?" I ask as he pays for our meal.

"Sounds great."

The night is perfect for riding—warm enough that the wind feels good against my skin, cool enough that pressing against him isn't uncomfortable.

Instead of heading back down the mountain, he turns onto a winding road that hugs the ridge line. The moon hangs low and full, painting the valley in silver light. Each curve opens up new views—the twinkling lights of town below, the dark expanse of forest, the silver ribbon of river cutting through it all.

The bike purrs between my thighs as we ride, powerful and controlled. Hawk handles it like it's an extension of himself, taking each curve with precision that speaks of years of experience. I find myself relaxing into the rhythm of it, letting my body move with his as we carve through the night.

We pass the old fire tower, its skeletal frame stark against the star-filled sky. The road narrows, trees pressing closer on either side, their branches forming a canopy overhead.

Moonlight filters through the leaves, creating shifting patterns on the asphalt.

Hawk slows as we approach a break in the trees, pulling off onto a small turnout. The valley spreads out below us, wider here than at the restaurant's viewpoint. The lights of three towns dot the darkness, connected by thin ribbons of highway.

"Beautiful, isn't it?" he asks as he kills the engine.

I stay where I am, still pressed against his back, my arms around his waist. "Worth the detour."

His hand covers mine where it rests on his stomach. "You haven't seen anything yet."

He's right. As my eyes adjust to the darkness, more details emerge. The silhouette of mountains against the star-filled sky. The movement of clouds across the moon. A shooting star streaks across the horizon, and I catch my breath.

"Make a wish," he murmurs.

I snort. "That's not very badass of you."

His laugh rumbles through his chest. "I contain multitudes, little lamb."

I close my eyes.

What do you wish for when your entire life has been turned upside down in the span of a week? For Amanda to come back? For her to stay gone? For money? For time? For answers?

I think of the kids—Abby's determined little frown when she's concentrating, Amy's belly laugh when she's truly happy, Adam's gummy smile. They deserve so much more than what life has given them.

Strength. I wish for strength. Strength to be what they need, to build them the life they deserve, to not screw this up the way everyone else in their lives has.

Hawk helps me off his bike, then turns us until he's half-seated, half leaning against it, with me wrapped in his arms, my back to his front.

We sit there for a while, neither of us speaking. The night wraps around us like a blanket—crickets chirping in the underbrush, a distant owl calling, the soft whisper of wind through pine needles. The rest of the world feels very far away.

Slowly, his warmth seeps into me, grounding and overwhelming.

I'm not used to this—the weight of someone else's care. It's terrifying how easy it would be to sink into him, to let him shoulder just a little of the burden I carry.

But that isn't fair, is it? To expect a man I've known for less than a week to wade into my chaos when I can barely keep my own head above water?

His hands rest lightly on my arms, his touch warm and steady.

"You overthinking again?" he murmurs, his voice low enough to blend with the whisper of the wind through the trees.

I swallow hard. "No."

"Liar." His tone teases, but his hold tightens just enough to make me feel anchored.

Safe.

That's the problem. The safety he offers is a mirage. Nothing about Hawk is safe. Not the way he looks at me, like I'm the only thing in his world that matters. Not the way he touches me, like he can't help himself. And certainly not the way he makes me feel—seen in a way I'm not sure I want to be.

I should pull away. Tell him this is a mistake. Put distance between us before I let myself believe, even for a second, that this can be anything other than a fleeting distraction.

But I don't.

Instead, I let myself relax into him, just for a beat. I let myself feel the solid strength of him at my back, the rise and fall of his breath matching mine. I let myself believe, if only for tonight, that I'm not alone.

The stars stretch endlessly above us, their cold light a stark contrast to the warmth between us. The moment feels fragile, like a bubble that might burst if I move too quickly or say the wrong thing.

"You ever just stop and look at the stars?" he asks, his voice breaking the silence but not the spell.

I tilt my head back, letting my eyes follow the trail of his gaze.

"Not really," I admit. "Too much to do. Too many things to worry about."

"You should." His hand shifts, his thumb tracing a slow, deliberate circle on my arm. "They remind you how small your problems really are."

I turn my head slightly, catching his profile in the moonlight. "Is that supposed to make me feel better?"

"Depends. Does it?"

I think about it—the overwhelming list of responsibilities waiting for me back home. The bills, the kids, the ache of trying to hold it all together. But here, wrapped in Hawk's arms with the stars above us and the world below, it all seems just a little more manageable. A little less crushing.

"Maybe," I admit.

I feel his breath against my neck, warm and teasing. His lips graze my skin, crawling up to my ear.

"Guess we'll have to take another ride and do some more stargazing," he says, his voice rough with something I can't quite name.

And just like that, the bubble bursts. Because it's too much—too intense, too real. And I'm a stupid girl for even considering putting my trust in a biker.

I can feel him watching me, like he can read what's going through my mind–all the thoughts and arguments as to why this is a terrible idea.

I pull away, stepping out of his embrace, and turn toward the bike.

"We should head back," I say, my voice cool.

Hawk doesn't argue, doesn't push. But as he starts the engine and I climb back on behind him, I know something has shifted between us.

"Ready?" he asks finally, his thumb tracing circles on my wrist.

No. Yes. Maybe.

"Yeah," I mutter, pressing my face to his cut. "Let's go."

He squeezes my hand once before starting the bike.

I tilt my head up to the sky, letting the stars blur in my vision, the cold wind biting at my cheeks. And then, without warning, a single tear slips free. It trails down my face, cold and foreign, as if my body is purging something I didn't even know I've been holding on to.

Is it relief? Grief? Or just the weight of everything crashing down at once? I don't know. But I let it fall, swallowed by the wind before I can wipe it away.

Hawk doesn't say anything, doesn't even look back. But somehow, I feel like he knows. Like he understands in the way he holds steady, his body a quiet, unspoken promise between us.

When we finally pull up to the house, all the windows glow warmly. Through the front window, I see Ginger sprawled on the couch reading, while Tank dozes in the armchair, his boots propped on the coffee table.

"Thanks for the ride," I say, my voice steady, even if I'm not.

Hawk's gaze lingers on me, sharp and assessing, and for a moment, I think he might say something. But then he just nods, his lips curving into a slow, knowing smile.

"Anytime, little lamb."

Hawk's hand finds the small of my back as we walk up the porch steps, the touch sending tingles up my spine despite the layers between his skin and mine.

The house is quiet except for the soft murmur of the TV and Tank's gentle snoring.

Ginger looks up from her book, a knowing smile crossing her face. "They were angels," she says before I can ask. "Even got Adam down without a fuss. Though Steel might need therapy after the tea party makeover."

"Where's Steel?" I ask, noting his absence.

"Sent him to bed. Apparently playing with toddlers all night is a bit too much for his manly constitution." She stretches, catlike. "Tank, baby, wake up. Time to go."

Tank grumbles but hauls himself up, dropping a kiss on Ginger's head. They gather their things with the easy familiarity of a long-term couple, and I feel that pang again—that dangerous whisper of wanting.

"Thanks for watching them," I say softly as they head for the door.

Ginger's smile is gentle. "Anytime, sugar. Really." She pulls me in for a warm hug, holding me tight and squeezing me. She smells like vanilla and orange blossom. I stiffen, surprised by the gesture before awkwardly returning her embrace.

She pulls back with a knowing smile, giving me a wink.

Once they're gone, the house feels different. Quieter. More intimate. Hawk's presence behind me seems to fill every inch of space, making it hard to breathe.

"I should check on them," I whisper, already moving

toward the hallway. I need to see them, to ground myself after the surreal evening.

The twins' room is bathed in the soft glow of their nightlight. They're curled together in one bed as they always end up, dark curls splayed across their pillows, tiny hands linked even in sleep. In the crib, Adam sleeps peacefully, one tiny fist pressed against his cheek.

I feel Hawk before I hear him, a solid warmth at my back. He stays where he is, giving me space while somehow making me aware of every inch between us.

"They're good kids," he says softly.

"Yeah." I turn, finding him leaning against the doorframe, his expression unreadable in the dim light. "They are."

He moves then, closing the distance between us with deliberate steps. His hand comes up, callused fingers brushing my cheek with surprising gentleness.

"You're good with them," he murmurs.

"I try to be." I swallow hard, fighting the urge to lean into his touch. "They deserve that."

"So do you."

Before I can process that, his mouth is on mine. This kiss is different from our first—slower, deeper, like he's trying to memorize the taste of me. His hands frame my face, thumbs stroking my cheeks as he draws me closer.

I let myself sink into him, let myself believe that this can be simple, uncomplicated. That I can have this without consequences, without fear. That the strength I've wished for might include the courage to let someone in.

But nothing in my life has ever been simple.

I pull back, walking on unsteady legs toward my bedroom door. "I should get some sleep."

"Andi." My name is rough in his throat, laden with things unsaid.

I pause in the doorway, one hand on the frame. The words come out before I can stop them, raw and honest in the darkness. "You know what's funny? It's easier to kiss you than it is to trust you."

I glance over to see the impact of my words in his eyes, in the way his jaw tightens, but I step through and close the bedroom door before he can respond.

Leaning against the wood, I touch my lips where I can still feel his kiss, wondering if any wall will be strong enough to keep him out.

Wondering if I want it to.

Damn.

11

HAWK

Duck's office is a cluttered sanctuary of old-school grit and stubborn independence. The walls are a patchwork of grease-stained posters, faded photos of muscle cars, and a calendar stuck on a year long past. A battered desk dominates the small room, its surface littered with a mismatched collection of tools, unpaid bills, and a half-empty bottle of whiskey that's likely seen more action than the coffee mug beside it. A fan in the corner sputters noisily, barely stirring the warm, oil-scented air, while the overhead light flickers faintly, casting uneven shadows across the floor.

The leather chair behind the desk creaks under Duck's weight, worn patches and scuffed arms telling tales of countless late nights spent balancing books and fending off threats to his little slice of turf. A stack of faded blueprints leans precariously against a filing cabinet, and the faint hum of a radio playing classic rock fills the silence when conversations die. Despite the chaos, the space has a certain charm—gritty, no-nonsense, and unapologetically Duck.

The fact he's called Axel and me in doesn't bode well.

"Got this earlier today." Duck tosses the envelope onto his desk. "Two million. Cash."

Axel whistles low, picking up the offer letter. "That's a lot of green for a garage in this neighborhood."

"That's because it ain't about the garage." I study Duck's face. The old timer is pissed. "Summit wants the land."

"Bingo." Duck drops into his chair, the leather groaning under his weight. "Got a visit yesterday. Real smooth talker in an expensive suit. Said the neighborhood's 'evolving.' That I should get out while the getting's good."

"Sounds gentle enough," Axel says, his tone light.

"Oh, it wasn't." Duck pulls a second bottle of whiskey from his bottom drawer, not bothering with glasses as he takes a swig. "Mentioned how it'd be a shame if the city found code violations. How insurance rates are going up in 'high-risk areas.'"

I catch the bottle he tosses my way. "Same playbook they're using on the residents."

"Yep." Duck leans forward, his chair creaking. "But here's what's got me thinking—they're moving too fast. Three months ago, they weren't even in town. Now they're throwing around millions like it's nothing."

"Money like that doesn't appear overnight," I say, rolling the bottle between my palms. "Not clean money, anyway. Those rumors about the cartel might be closer to the truth than we thought."

Axel moves to the window, watching the garage floor below. "Lee says they're bringing in workers from out of state. Whole crews. Setting up temp housing at the old factory site."

"Before permits?" Duck's eyebrows shoot up.

"That's the thing." Axel turns back to us. "Permits are flying through city hall. Projects that should take months to approve are getting rubber-stamped in days."

"The mayor's been spotted at the country club with Summit's CEO," I add. "Real cozy from what our prospects report."

Duck snorts. "Roberts wouldn't know honest money if it bit him in the ass. But still—why here? Why now?"

"Location." Axel pulls out his phone, bringing up a map. "Look at it. Highway access. Rail line runs right behind the neighborhood. And those old mining tunnels underneath—"

"Perfect for moving things you don't want found," I finish.

"Exactly." Axel's face is grim. "Plus, they're targeting specific properties. The Wilson place? Old factory? Duck's garage? They form a corridor."

"A pipeline," Duck mutters. "Jesus."

"But for what?" I stand, restless energy making it hard to sit still. "Drugs? Weapons?"

"Whatever it is, they need it done fast." Axel traces the route on his phone. "They're not just buying properties—they're isolating them. Utilities getting cut, road work blocking access, health code violations appearing out of nowhere."

"Wearing people down," Duck says. "Making them desperate to sell."

"Making them disappear," I correct. "No witnesses, no questions."

The office falls silent except for the sputtering fan and the distant sound of engines being worked on. Through the window, I see Andi bent over a motorcycle, her movements precise and focused.

"Your girl's place is right in their path," Duck says quietly.

"She's not my—" I stop at Duck's knowing look. "I know."

"They'll come for her next," Axel warns. "Put pressure on the landlord."

"I've got it covered."

"You better," Duck says grimly. He pulls another envelope from his desk. "Had my lawyer draw up these papers this morning. Transferring forty-nine percent ownership of the garage to the club."

I stare at the papers Duck's tossed on the desk. Forty-nine percent. He's giving up control of something he's built from nothing.

"Duck—" I start.

He holds up a hand. "Before either of you start, this ain't charity. And I'm not retiring." He jerks his thumb toward the garage floor. "Got too many projects. Too many good people depending on this place."

"Why now?" Axel asks, picking up the papers.

"Because I'm not stupid." Duck leans back, the chair groaning in protest. "Summit's got reach. Deep pockets. If something happens to me—"

"Nothing's going to happen," I cut in sharply.

"If something happens," Duck continues, ignoring me, "Maggie'd be left holding the bag. She's tough as nails, but she shouldn't have to deal with their kind of pressure."

Axel scans the documents, his expression thoughtful. "Split ownership makes it harder to sell. They'd need club approval."

"And we don't approve shit without a vote," I add, already seeing where this is going.

"Exactly." Duck's eyes crinkle. "Plus, gives me an excuse to keep you idiots in line. Make sure my investment's protected."

I snort. As if Duck needs an excuse to bust our balls.

"There's more." He pulls out another set of papers. "Been thinking about expanding. That lot next door's been empty since the hardware store went under. Could double our workspace, add more bays."

"Add more mechanics," Axel says slowly. "More eyes on the street. We'll need to get in before Summit."

Duck nods. "I already put in an offer last week."

I study the old-timer, impressed despite myself. He's thought this through.

"Stone know about this?" I ask.

"Called him this morning. He's on board, pending club vote." Duck's expression turns serious. "Look, boys. This garage? It's more than just a business. It's family. Community. People come here when they need help, not just with their cars."

I turn away, watching one of the junior mechanics showing Andi something on an engine. She laughs, rubbing a hand across her forehead before bending over to point something out.

The sight of her hits me like a physical blow—both the curve of her ass in those coveralls and her easy joy. Her laugh hasn't been directed at me since that night on my bike.

Christ, that ride.

She'd felt perfect pressed against my back, her thighs gripping mine, her arms wound tight around my waist. I remember how she'd let down her guard just for a moment. How she'd allowed me to glimpse who she was underneath the walls she'd erected so high.

Those fucking walls. I'd give anything to tear them down, to find the woman underneath all that ice and independence. To be the one she lets in, the one she learns to trust.

Watching her now, laughing with someone else, strikes something possessive in my chest. It's more than just wanting her body, though God knows I do. I want her smiles, her trust, her heart. Want to be the one she turns to, the one who gets to see her soft and unguarded.

But she's got three kids depending on her, a life she's carved out on her own terms. She doesn't need some biker with too much baggage complicating things.

Except... maybe that's exactly what she needs. Someone to share the load, to have her back, to love those kids like they deserve. Someone to show her she doesn't have to do it all alone.

I could be that someone. If she'd let me.

The thought should terrify me. Instead, it feels right. Like pieces clicking into place.

"...more than just a business," Duck is saying, his words pulling me back to the conversation. "It's family. Community. People come here when they need help, not just with their cars."

He shook his head. "Summit doesn't understand this community. They see property values, development opportunities. They don't see the lives they're trying to destroy."

"We won't let them," Axel says firmly.

"Damn straight." Duck pulls out three glasses from his bottom drawer, pouring a measure of whiskey in each—guess we're done with drinking straight from the bottle.

"You didn't bring us here just for this," I say, turning to look at him. "What do you need from us?"

He chuckles. "Sharp as a tack. You're right. Stone wants you and Axel to lead the project." He slides the glasses across the desk. "You boys in?"

I pick up the whiskey, thinking about everything this place means. About the people who depend on it. About a certain mechanic who's carved out her own place here.

"Fuck it," I say.

Axel raises his glass. "To family."

"To fighting dirty," Duck adds with a grin.

"To riding free."

We clink glasses, then drink deep.

"Now," Duck says, settling back in his chair. "Make yourself useful and give Andi this." He shoves a clipboard with papers across the desk. "And for god's sake, pull your head out of your ass and claim her. I've worked too hard on that girl for you to fuck it up."

I raise an eyebrow. "You've worked too hard?"

Duck snorts. "Three years, I've watched that girl rebuild herself. Started at the bottom, fought her way up. Never asked for help, never complained." He leans forward.

"You know how many guys in this town tried to get her attention? How many assholes I had to run off?"

"That why you put her in the back bay?" Axel asks, grinning. "Protecting your investment?"

"Damn straight. Girl's got talent. Natural feel for engines you can't teach." Duck's expression turns serious. "But she's got trust issues."

I watch as Andi works, her movements precise and confident. "Can't blame her."

"No," Duck agrees. "But you can do something about it." He taps the clipboard. "These are the designs for the expansion. I want her opinion on the layout."

"Since when do you need opinions on garage layouts?"

Duck's eyes crinkle. "Since I decided to put her in charge of the restoration division."

That gets my attention. "You what?"

"She doesn't know yet." He holds up a hand before I can protest. "Was waiting for the right time. Figure now's as good as any, what with Summit breathing down our necks."

"She won't take charity," I warn.

"Ain't charity when she's the best person for the job." Duck's tone brooks no argument. "Look, you want to protect her? Give her a reason to stay. Something that's hers. Something worth fighting for."

"Besides three kids?" Axel ducks the pen I throw at his head.

"For fuck's sake." Duck shoves up from his chair and stomps across to the ancient coffee maker in the corner of his office. He pours some into a chipped mug and shoves it at me. "Here. Start with caffeine, then work your way up to the job offer."

"And declarations of undying love," Axel adds helpfully.

I shoot them both a look, but the bastards just grin.

"Go get your girl," Duck says softly. "Before someone decides to make her another kind of offer."

That sobers me. I take the coffee and clipboard, already planning my next move. I stand in the doorway of Duck's office for a moment, watching her work. She hasn't noticed me yet, too focused on the engine in front of her. Her hair's pulled back in a messy ponytail, grease streaks across one cheek, and her coveralls have seen better days.

She looks fucking beautiful.

I push off the doorframe and make my way over to her.

"Coffee delivery."

Her head snaps up, a smile starting before she catches herself. "You're not my usual coffee guy."

"He was busy." I hold out the mug. "Turns out the fucker's plotting world domination."

She takes the coffee, her fingers brushing mine. "Duck?

Plotting?" She snorts. "More like grumbling about paperwork."

If she only knew.

"Speaking of paperwork..." I hold up the clipboard.

"No." She turns back to the engine. "Whatever it is, no. I've got three builds to finish this week, not to mention dealing with the Vincent, helping Joe before his final apprenticeship test, and—"

"Duck's orders."

She pauses, wrench hovering over the cylinder head. "Since when are you Duck's errand boy?"

"Since he decided to make you head of restoration."

"Well, you can tell him to go get—wait. What did you say?"

I hold out the clipboard. "Plans for the expansion. He wants your input on the layout since you'll be in charge of restorations."

She doesn't take it. "This is a joke."

"No joke, little lamb." I step closer, into her space. "You've earned this."

"I haven't—" She swallows hard. "I can't—"

"Can't what? Run the best restoration department in three states? Because that's what Duck's planning." I tap the clipboard against her chest. "He thinks you can do it. I think you can do it."

"You don't even know me," she whispers.

"Don't I?" I catch her chin, lifting it until she meets my eyes. "I know you work harder than anyone here. I know you've got talent Duck says he hasn't seen in thirty years. I know you'd do anything for those kids."

"The kids..." Her eyes widen. "Oh god, the kids. I can't take on more responsibility when—"

"When what? When you're already proving you can handle anything life throws at you?" My thumb brushes a grease mark on her cheek. "Take the job, Andi. Build something for yourself. For them."

She stares at me for a long moment, something vulnerable flickering in her eyes. Then she steps back, breaking contact.

"Why do you care?" she asks softly.

The question hangs between us, heavy and raw, like the tension in the room might snap if either of us moves too fast. Andi's voice is soft, but there's an edge to it, like she isn't sure if she wants the answer or if it'll cut deeper than the silence already has. Her gaze pins me in place, searching for something—truth, maybe, or just a reason to trust what I've said.

I exhale slowly, running a hand through my hair, the weight of her vulnerability making it hard to speak. "Because someone has to," I finally say, my voice low. "Because... I know what it's like to feel like the whole world's ready to let you fall."

Her lips press together, but she doesn't look away. For a second, I think she might, but then she just stands there, like she's bracing herself against the storm my words stir inside her.

"Andi, I've seen what you can do," I say. "With engines. With the kids. With..." *Me.* "Take the plans. Look them over. Think about Duck's offer."

She takes the clipboard slowly, like it might bite. "I'll think about it."

"Good." I back away before I do something stupid like kiss her in the middle of the garage. "Oh, and babe?"

"Not your babe."

I grin. "Sweetheart, you've got grease on your face."

Her hand flies to her cheek, smearing it worse. "Damn it, why didn't you—"

I chuckle, walking away before she can respond, her spluttering following me out. But not before I catch her small smile as she glances down at the plans.

First wall down. Now for the rest.

12

HAWK

She's been avoiding me all week.

Not obviously—Andi's too smart for that. But suddenly, she's always busy when I'm home. Always surrounded by kids, prospects, or Ginger when our paths cross.

It's driving me fucking crazy.

"You're brooding again," Axel says, handing me a beer as we watch the party start to fill the backyard. "It's not attractive."

"Fuck off."

He grins, leaning against the deck railing beside me. "She'll come around."

"Who said anything about—"

"The way you've been watching the front door for the last

hour?" He takes a pull from his beer. "Dead giveaway, brother."

I don't bother denying it. The club started arriving early, bikes filling the street as the sun sets. Music thumps from speakers someone set up in the garage, and the smell of grilling meat fills the air. A normal Saturday night gathering.

Except nothing feels normal anymore.

"Where are the kids?" Axel asks.

"Duck and Maggie's." I try not to think about how empty the house feels without them. Without her. "Sleepover with their grandkids."

"Convenient."

I shoot him a look that would have prospects pissing themselves. Axel just grins wider.

Movement by the gate catches my attention. Ginger's here, and with her...

"Damn," Axel mutters.

Andi's in dark jeans that hug curves I've been dreaming about all week, and a top that shows more skin than I've seen since that first kiss. Her hair is down, falling in waves past her shoulders, and Ginger's clearly gotten to her with makeup.

She looks fucking beautiful. And completely untouchable.

"Well," Axel pushes off the railing, "this should be interesting."

I watch as Ginger leads Andi through the crowd, collecting women as they go. Tank's old lady presses a beer into Andi's hand, and even from here, I see her hesitate before taking it.

"Good," Axel says. "Girl needs to relax."

"Since when do you care?"

He shrugs. "Since she started making you less of an asshole."

I don't have a response to that.

The night wears on, the party getting louder as more people arrive. I keep my distance, watching as Andi slowly relaxes into the atmosphere. She keeps nursing her original beer, picking at the label.

The women claim a corner of the garage as their dance floor, and even from my spot on the deck, I see Andi starting to move with the music.

"You gonna stand there all night?" Stone appears beside me, his timing as impeccable as always.

"Maybe."

He snorts. "Kids are fine, by the way."

"How do you know that?"

"Called Duck to check in on club shit. All I heard was fucking screaming."

That gets a laugh out of me. "He knew what he was signing up for."

"Did you?"

I turn to find my President watching me with knowing eyes.

"She'd make a good old lady," he says quietly. "She's solid. Keeps her head. You want her. We'll support you."

The music changes, something slower and darker threading through the night. Through the crowd, I see Andi dancing with Ginger, her movements loose and free in a way I've never seen before.

"Yeah," I admit. "She is."

Stone claps me on the shoulder. "Then do something about it."

"She's avoiding me."

"Can you blame her? Girl's whole life has blown up, and here you come riding in like a knight in tarnished armor."

I snort, tearing my gaze from Andi. "You're a prick, you know that, right?"

Stone's smile is knowing. "Stop being chickenshit."

Shit.

"Go get your girl," he says softly. "Life's too fucking short. Don't regret decisions you shouldn't have made."

There's a weight to his words, a grief behind them.

I watch as Andi throws her head back, laughing at something Ginger says. The sight hits me like a punch to the gut.

As if sensing my gaze, Andi's eyes meet mine across the crowd. For a moment, neither of us looks away. Then Ginger grabs her hand, spinning her into another dance, and the connection breaks.

But something shifts.

I watch as she makes her way to the makeshift bar, finally ditching her warm beer for a fresh one. The party has hit that sweet spot where inhibitions start to fall away—couples grinding on the dance floor, prospects trying to impress sweet butts, old-timers telling war stories by the grill.

And Andi, moving through it all like she belongs here. Like she's always belonged here.

The song changes again, something with a heavy bass that vibrates through the ground. Ginger squeals, grabbing Andi's hand.

"This is my song!"

I can't hear Andi's response over the music, but her laugh carries.

Tank appears beside me, watching his old lady dance. "Gorgeous, isn't she?"

"Yeah." But I'm not looking at Ginger.

Andi moves like she works—with precision, with confidence, with a grace that draws the eye. Her hips sway to the beat, and I find myself wondering how they'd feel under my hands.

She lifts her arms up, moving to the music with her eyes closed. Her shirt rides up, showing a strip of skin above her jeans. My mouth goes dry as I stare at all her curvy, generous, soft skin.

"Fuck it," I mutter, pushing off the railing.

Stone's laugh follows me as I carve my way through the crowd. People move aside, some with knowing grins, others too drunk to notice. The music gets louder as I approach the women's corner, the bass thumping in time with my pulse.

Ginger sees me coming, her grin wicked as she spins Andi around, positioning her perfectly.

One step.

Two.

She backs right into me.

Her body goes rigid for a moment before she realizes who it is. Then something else entirely takes over.

"Hawk," she breathes, not quite turning around.

My hands find her hips, holding her in place. "Dance with me."

It's not a request. We both know it.

She stays facing forward, but her body melts back into mine as the music wraps around us. My hands tighten on her hips, guiding her movements to match mine.

Around us, the party fades to background noise. All I can focus on is the way she moves against me, the scent of her hair, the heat of her skin under my palms.

"You've been avoiding me," I say, low enough that only she can hear.

"Yes." No denial, no excuses. Just honesty.

"Why?"

She turns in my arms, finally meeting my eyes. The motion brings us chest to chest, and my grip shifts to her lower back.

"You scare me," she admits.

"How?"

Her hands come up to rest on my chest. "The way you look at me. The way you are with the kids." She swallows hard. "The way you make me want things I shouldn't."

That's bullshit. She shouldn't want for anything.

"What do you want?"

"This." She presses closer, her body moving with mine as the music shifts to something slower, darker. "You make me believe we might be possible."

"We are." I slide one hand up her back, feeling her shiver.

"Hawk—"

"Andi, dance with me," I cut her off. "No talking, no doubts, no overthinking. Tonight, just let me hold you."

Something in her eyes softens. Her fingers curl into my shirt as she nods.

So we dance.

Her body moves against mine like we've done this a thousand times before. Every movement, every touch, builds something between us that feels inevitable. Unstoppable.

When her head tips forward to rest on my chest, I know I'm lost.

"I'm tired of denying this," she whispers against my shirt.

My arms tighten around her. "Then don't."

She lifts her head, meeting my eyes. The vulnerability there hits me like a physical blow.

"Take me inside," she says softly.

Two hours of watching her dance, days of her avoiding me, over a week of wanting her—it all crashes together in that moment.

"You sure?"

Her smile is everything I've been waiting for.

"Take me to bed, Hawk."

She doesn't have to ask twice.

13

ANDI

The party still pulses outside, but in Hawk's bedroom, everything feels different. Quieter. More intense.

He doesn't rush me, doesn't push. He just leads me through the house with his hand on my lower back, the heat of his touch burning through my shirt. Now he stands watching me, giving me space to change my mind.

I don't want to change my mind.

"I can hear you thinking," he says softly.

"Bad habit." I manage a smile. "Occupational hazard."

He crosses to me slowly, like I might startle. "Want to tell me what's going on in that head of yours?"

I look up at him, at this man who somehow becomes the center of my world without me noticing. The man who makes pancakes for the twins and rocks Adam to sleep.

The man who looks at me like I'm something precious instead of something broken.

"I'm scared," I admit.

His hands come up to frame my face. "Of what?"

"Everything." I swallow hard.

"Do you trust me?"

"Yes." The admission costs me something, but his smile makes it worth it.

"Come here."

He kisses me like he has all night, like we have all the time in the world. His hands slide into my hair as he draws me closer, and I let myself melt into him.

This is different from our other kisses. Those had been stolen moments, charged with tension and uncertainty. This... this feels like coming home.

"Been thinking about this all week," he murmurs against my lips.

"That why you kept stopping by the shop?"

His laugh rumbles through his chest. "Guilty."

I slide my hands under his shirt, needing to feel his skin. He's all hard muscle and heated flesh, and the sound he makes when my nails scrape lightly across his stomach sends heat pooling low in my belly.

"Off," I demand, tugging at the fabric.

He complies, pulling back just long enough to strip off his shirt. I haven't seen him shirtless before, and now that I do, I feel like I've been granted all my Christmas wishes at once.

His broad chest is a masterpiece of lean muscle and intricate ink—dark lines flow across his left pectoral and down his ribs, while a skull wraps around his right shoulder. Stoneheart MC is branded on his skin, marking him as a lifer.

I like it. I like that he's committed. That he belongs.

While the tattoos are a roadmap I want to explore, right now, I just want him.

"Your turn," he growls, fingers finding the hem of my top.

I hesitate only a moment before lifting my arms. The fabric whispers over my skin, and then I'm standing in just my bra, feeling exposed.

"Beautiful," he breathes, hands spanning my waist. "So fucking beautiful."

No one has ever looked at me like this—like I'm something to be cherished rather than used. Like my curves are perfect instead of too much.

"Hawk—"

"I've got you." He pulls me close, skin to skin. "I've got you, little lamb."

For the first time in my life, I let myself believe it.

His mouth finds mine again as we move toward the bed. Clothes fall away between kisses, between touches that grow increasingly desperate. When he finally slides into me, I gasp his name.

"Look at me," he demands softly.

I open my eyes, finding his locked on mine.

"Stay with me," he says. "Right here. With me."

I nod, unable to look away as he begins to move. Everything else falls away—the party outside, my fears. There's only this, only him, only us.

I arch into his touch, needing more, craving more. He obliges, his mouth trailing fire down my neck, across my collarbones, lower still to take one aching nipple between his lips. I cry out, my fingers sinking into his hair to hold him in place. The scrape of his beard against my skin is a delicious contrast to the wet heat of his mouth.

"Hawk, please..." I don't know what I'm begging for, only that I need it, need him.

"Please what?" he murmurs against my skin.

His touch is gentle—reverent almost—as his hands map my curves. The way he touches me makes me feel beautiful. Cherished.

I meet his gaze, seeing something there that makes my chest tight. No one has ever looked at me like this—like I am precious, like I matter.

"You're everything," he whispers, pressing his forehead to mine.

I wrap my arms around him, pulling him closer, needing to feel his warmth, his strength, his steadiness. His heartbeat thunders against my palm where it rests on his chest, matching my own racing pulse.

The moment stretches between us, heavy with meaning. Then he kisses me—slow and deep and perfect—and I stop thinking altogether.

His hands tangle in my hair as he angles my head, deepening the kiss. His other hand slips under my shirt, skimming up my spine and sending shivers dancing across my skin.

I moan into his mouth, arching into his touch.

He pulls away, gasping for air. "God, Andi..."

I lean up on my elbows, tracing a finger along his jawline. "Good?"

He grins. "Perfect."

"Excellent," I say breathlessly, tugging him lower again. "Because I'm not done with you yet."

I don't know how much longer I can take this torture. Hawk's mouth is a drug, his touch pure fire, and with every second that passes, my control frays that little bit more.

"Condom," I manage to whimper.

He pulls back, holding eye contact as he reaches for his bedside drawer. Our fingers brush as he hands it over, a shock of electricity sizzling between us.

"Put it on me," he commands softly.

His eyes rake over me, dark and hungry, and my legs clench in response.

God, I am wet. So fucking wet.

Slowly, I unbutton his jeans, my gaze never leaving his. I can see the feral need in him, the way he fights for control as I tease him.

I free him from his pants, licking my lips nervously as I gaze down at the fistful of cock I've revealed. He is average size but thick, so thick I know he'll need to stretch me before being able to work his way inside.

"Can I taste?" I ask, holding his cock in one hand, the condom in the other.

His rumbled reply is lost as he bunches his fingers in my hair and gently pushes me down.

My tongue swirls around the head of his cock, his groaned appreciation shooting lightning through me.

"Fuck."

"Too much?" I ask, looking up at him with a cheeky grin.

"Never."

I smirk and oblige, taking more of him into my mouth. He clenches his fists in the bedsheets as I explore— teasing him with long, slow laps of my tongue, gently stroking my nails down his shaft.

"Fuck it." Hawk jackknifes into a seat, slipping his arms under me. In a move so smooth and effective I can't help but be impressed, he has me flipped until my pussy is directly above his face, my mouth over his cock.

"Better?" I ask, shooting him a grin over my shoulder. His answer is to plunge his face into me, his greedy mouth finding my clit.

Then it is my turn to groan.

With a muffled chuckle, he sets to work, his tongue lapping at my sensitive nubbin, sending me into a tailspin of pleasure.

Arching my back, I ride his face, grinding my hips against his mouth as he chases the sensations he creates. I grip his cock, jerking it as I pant, utterly destroyed by his hands which are everywhere. He strokes my thighs, cups my breasts, and tweaks my nipples, allowing no space to recover.

"Harder," I gasp.

He complies, his tongue lapping at my entrance as he pushes two fingers inside me.

With a moan, I fall upon his cock, sucking him deep. He tastes salty against my tongue, filling my mouth and throat as I suck him, working his shaft with my hands.

Desperation drives us, each fighting to make the other lose control first.

"Fuck, Andi." Hawk groans. "You taste so fucking good."

I gasp in response, my pussy clenching around his fingers as my orgasm builds. I pull back, rolling the condom down his shaft as he works me.

"Want you inside me."

"Not yet," he croons. "Come first."

His tongue resumes its tortured pleasure as his words tip me over. I scream his name as I come apart.

I release his cock to brace myself against his legs, grinding against his face, desperate to draw out my release.

His hands wrap around my thick thighs, holding me against him. He grunts, pleasurable sounds that feed my desire.

He is so good, so fucking good.

"Fuck, Andi."

That is all the warning I get before he pulls away and flips me over, pinning me to the bed.

His eyes blaze with hunger and something else—something darker, more primal.

He doesn't give me time to process, sliding his cock first against me then into me, working his length until my tight, protesting muscles force him to stop.

I gasp, my pussy clenching around him as he stretches me, waits for me to adjust to his girth.

He groans, burrowing his face in the crook of my neck. "Fuck, you feel so tight. Let me work you a little more."

I can only whimper in response, pleasure unraveling like a tightly coiled spring.

"I've wanted you for so fucking long," he grinds out between clenched teeth.

I huff out a laugh. "You've known me for less than two weeks."

"Exactly."

He pulls back, working into me in small shallow thrusts. I arch my hips, trying to pull him deeper despite the slight pain.

"Hurry," I pant, clutching at him.

His pace doesn't falter. "I'm being slow," he growls.

"But I need more."

He chuckles as he clips his hips forward again, causing me to moan. "Tell me what you want me to do."

I can feel the tension building again, coiling in my stomach and lower down. I grab his ass, extracting a low moan from him as he picks up the pace. "Faster, harder."

He catches my mouth in a feral kiss. His tongue moves against mine as he thrusts within me, one hand tangling in my hair while the other grips my hip.

Every touch feels like he is trying to memorize me, learn every curve, every response.

"That's it," he murmurs against my lips. "Let me hear you."

My nails rake down his back as pleasure builds between us. The weight of him above me, the strength in his arms as he holds himself up, the way his muscles move under my hands—it is overwhelming in the best way.

"You feel so good," he groans, his rhythm faltering slightly.

I tighten my legs around him, drawing him deeper. The new angle has us both moaning.

"Hawk," I gasp. "I need—"

"I know what you need." His hand slides between us, finding exactly the right spot. "Come for me, little lamb. Let go."

The endearment, spoken in that rough voice, pushes me over the edge. I shatter around him, his name a cry on my lips. He follows moments later, burying his face in my neck as he groans my name.

He collapses onto me, his weight deliciously heavy.

We lay there, panting as our breathing evens out. His still-hard cock lies between us, the condom a reminder of what has just transpired.

With a groan, Hawk rolls off me and onto his side, pulling me into him. Exhausted, I allow him to hold me, curling against his chest. Our breathing slows, the sweat on our skin cooling.

With a sigh, I make to move but am stopped by his arms that clamp tight around me.

"Where you going?"

I glance up at him. "To bed."

"You're already in bed."

"I meant my bed."

"Babe." Hawk squeezes his arms, holding me in place. "Stay."

My eyebrows rise. "Really?"

"Mm." He pulls me in for a kiss. "Don't read into it. I just want to be able to fuck you later."

I chuckle, shoving his face away playfully. "What an offer."

His arms tighten around me. "Seriously, Andi. Stay."

I lift my head to meet his eyes, seeing in them everything I'd been afraid to want.

"Okay. Just for tonight."

His sly grin steals my breath.

"We'll see."

14

ANDI

"Higher!" Abby squeals, her little legs pumping as Hawk pushes her on the swing.

"Higher!" Amy echoes from the swing beside her, not to be outdone.

"Any higher and you'll flip over the top," Hawk warns, but he gives them both another gentle push.

I watch from the picnic blanket, Adam sleeping against my chest, as my tiny daredevils reach for the sky. The park is quiet this early, morning sun filtering through the trees, dew still clinging to the grass.

This has become our Sunday ritual—early morning park visits before the crowds, followed by pancakes at home. The twins live for it. And watching Hawk with them...

"Penny for your thoughts?" he asks, dropping onto the blanket beside me as the girls run off to climb over the slide.

"Just thinking how good you are with them."

His smile is soft as he reaches out to stroke Adam's cheek. The baby snuffles in his sleep but doesn't wake.

"They make it easy," he says. He leans in to kiss me, his hand slipping under my shirt to tease the skin at my hip.

Two weeks of living in Hawk's house, of sleeping in his bed, of sharing childcare and meals, of making love deep into the night.

It feels like a dream.

I'd tried to create space between us the morning after, but Hawk refused to have it. And my effort to shut him out had resulted with him sneaking into my bedroom in the middle of the night to wake me with deep, addicting kisses.

We break apart laughing as the girls abandon the play equipment to pile onto the blanket.

"Hungry!" Abby announces, crawling into Hawk's lap.

"Pahcakes?" Amy asks hopefully, snuggling into my side.

"Sandwiches," Hawk corrects firmly. "But first, I think someone needs changing."

Adam chooses that moment to wake, blinking up at us with his sweet baby smile.

"I got him." Hawk scoops him up with practiced ease. "Come on, little man. Let's get you sorted while these ladies pack up."

I watch him head for the restrooms, Adam's tiny hand patting his chest, and my heart feels too full.

Amy tugs my sleeve. "Choc-it?"

"Chocolate," I correct automatically. "And not until after lunch."

They run off, screaming around the park while I fold the blanket. By the time Hawk returns with a fresh, happy Adam, we are ready to head home.

The walk home is perfect chaos—twins racing ahead before stopping every few feet to examine rocks or flowers or particularly interesting leaves. Hawk carries Adam in one arm, his other hand linked with mine.

My cell rings as we get close to the house. I step away, taking it as Hawk wrangles the kids down the street.

"This is Andi speaking," I answer.

"Hi, Ms. Daniels, this is Miranda from Swift Utilities. I'm calling to confirm that your power and water are scheduled to be restored this afternoon. You should have full service by 3 PM."

"Thank you so much," I reply, relief mixing with something bittersweet. "I appreciate the update."

Hanging up, I hesitate for a moment, watching Hawk crouch to pick up a dandelion one of the twins holds out to him, a soft smile curving his lips.

"All good?" he asks when I rejoin him.

"Yeah, it was the utility company." I glance up at him. "The power and water will be back on today."

"That's good news," he says, his gaze steady on mine.

"Yeah," I echo, but my voice lacks the enthusiasm I think I should feel.

It is good news—great news, even. It means I can finally go home, settle back into my own space, and reclaim some normalcy. But the thought doesn't fill me with the relief I'd expected. Instead, it leaves me torn.

Living here, with Hawk and the kids, has been...amazing. Messy and loud, yes, but also warm and full in a way I hadn't realized I'd been missing.

We feel like a family. Even if it is only temporary.

"You thinking of moving back in?" he asks.

Before I can respond, Abby lets out a shriek of delight. I glance over, finding her and Amy following a butterfly.

"You should stay. The house would be too quiet without you," he says, his thumb tracing circles on my palm. "Plus, Steel would be heartbroken. Pretty sure he's got tea parties booked through next month."

I try to laugh around the lump in my throat.

"We can't," I say, my voice rough. "It's too much to ask of you."

"Psh." Hawk pulls me closer, adjusting Adam on his hip. "Stay. At least until you find a better place."

The offer is casual, but there is weight behind it. Two weeks of living together has changed things between us. Changed me. I am starting to trust this—trust him—in ways that should terrify me.

Maybe they still do, a little.

"You're sure?" I ask. "We're not exactly low maintenance."

He snorts. "Babe, the clubhouse has more toys than the department store, our fridge is covered in finger paintings, and I know three different ways to braid hair. Pretty sure we're past that conversation."

"True." I watch the twins chase each other in circles. "It's a lot, Hawk. I feel bad asking that of you, of the club."

"Nah." His grin is wicked. "What do you think prospects are for? Babysitting and cleaning."

We reach the house, the twins racing up the steps ahead of us. Through the window, I can see evidence of our invasion everywhere—sippy cups on the counter, stuffed animals on the couch, a half-finished puzzle on the coffee table.

It looks like home.

"So?" Hawk asks as we reach the porch. "You staying?"

I think about my apartment, sitting empty except for the few things we'd brought here. Think about the life I'd built there, careful and controlled and lonely.

Think about this man who makes pancakes for my kids and knows how to handle nightmares and never once makes me feel like we are a burden.

"Yeah," I say softly. "We're staying."

"Thank fuck," he murmurs, kissing my temple. "Thought I was gonna have to kidnap you."

"Kidnap me, huh?" I tease, cocking an eyebrow. "I bet you say that to all the girls."

"Nah, just the really pretty ones with kids."

Laughing, I slap his butt as I move to open the door. "Promises, promises."

15

HAWK

The call comes at just after midnight.

"We need you," Lee's voice is tight with tension. "Axel's caught up in some shit with Summit's guys. It's bad."

I am already moving, sliding from bed and reaching for my cut. Beside me, Andi stirs.

"Everything okay?" she mumbles, voice thick with sleep.

"Club business," I say, leaning down to kiss her forehead. "Go back to sleep. I'll be back soon."

She makes a soft sound of acknowledgment, already drifting off again. I watch her for a moment, memorizing the curve of her face.

Fuck she is beautiful. Feels good to have a woman like her next to me, in my bed, in my life.

More than I'd ever thought I'd deserve.

The night is thick with humidity, my bike's headlight cutting through fog as I ride to the meetup point. Lee is waiting with Tank and two prospects, their faces grim in the weak light of dawn.

"What happened?" I demand as I kill my engine.

"Axel was doing recon, when security showed up for an early shift change." Lee's jaw is tight. "He's stuck in the records room. They've changed their schedule. These guys look new and eager. They're doing rounds every fifteen minutes. He can't get out without being seen."

"Fuck." I study the building's layout on Lee's phone. "How many guards?"

"Four that we can see. Camera five is compromised." He taps his phone. "So we can get him in but getting him out is gonna be harder."

My phone buzzes—Andi. I hit ignore, focusing on the situation at hand.

"We need a distraction," I say. "Something to draw them away long enough for Axel to slip out."

The prospects nod eagerly. Young, dumb, and ready to prove themselves. Perfect.

"No violence," I warn. "Nothing that can be traced back to us. We're here to get our brother out, not tip these fuckers off that we're starting a war."

My phone vibrates again. Andi's face lighting up my screen.

"Fuck," I mutter, hitting ignore again. Whatever it is will have to wait.

We split up, the prospects heading to the far side of the complex with instructions to trigger some car alarms. Tank positions himself by the emergency exit while Lee and I work our way toward the security office.

My cell buzzes a third time.

"Jesus, Hawk, you wanna give our position away?"

Andi's call stops, only to start up once more. I hesitate, a rock settling in my gut. I don't have time to deal with her, Axel needs me.

My club needs me.

I hit decline and power off the cell, pushing away the guilt I feel.

The Summit's temporary building looms ahead, all white panels and steel wrapped in scaffolding. The three story-modular would house their operations over the next few years as they slowly corrode our town, buying up business and housing to create their pipeline.

I want to burn the fucking thing to the ground.

We slip through the shadows, using the construction equipment dotted across the grounds like sleeping giants as cover.

"There." Lee points to a second-floor window. Light flickers behind the blinds just once—Axel's signal.

I study the guards. They move with the rigid precision of ex-military, weapons visible on their hips. These aren't the usual rent-a-cops Summit usually hires.

"They're professionals," I mutter. "Summit's stepping up their game."

"Makes you wonder what Axel might have found in there," Lee replies.

The sound of boots on gravel has us pressing deeper into the shadows. A guard passes within feet of our position, radio crackling with updates from his team.

"Third floor clear," a voice reports. "Moving to records."

Fuck. They are closing in on Axel's position.

A metallic crash echoes from the far side of the building, followed by the wail of car alarms.

The prospects, right on schedule.

"All units, check the disturbance," the radio squawks. "Could be kids again."

"Negative," another voice cuts in. "Hold positions. Wilson, check it out."

Shit. These guys are good.

"Plan B," I growl to Lee. "Tank in position?"

Lee taps his earpiece. "He's ready when you say."

"You got a spare one of them?"

Lee hands it over. I study the building once more as I slip

it into my ear. We need something bigger. Something that would force them to investigate.

The construction site catches my eye. Specifically, the electrical junction box controlling the temporary lighting.

"New plan," I say. "Get Tank to the breaker box. When I give the signal, cut power to the whole block."

Lee's grin is feral in the darkness. "Create some chaos?"

"Exactly." I check my watch. "Axel's got eight minutes before the next sweep. We do this fast, clean, and quiet."

"And if they catch us?"

I think of the guns on their hips, the way they move like soldiers instead of security. "Don't get caught."

The night presses in around us as we move into position. Tank's shadow slips between the construction equipment while Lee makes his way to the emergency exit. The prospects have gone silent, waiting for the signal.

One shot at this. One chance to get it right.

I wait, watching for the perfect moment.

There.

One of the guards has bent to tie his shoelace.

I give the signal and the night explodes into chaos.

The block plunges into darkness as Tank hits the power. At the same instant, a series of car alarms begin screaming from the far lot, while the prospects throw what sounds like half a hardware store worth of metal pipes across the concrete.

"What the fuck?" a guard shouts. Flashlight beams cut through the darkness, dancing across the construction site.

"Control, we've lost power to the whole sector," another radios in. "Possible breach."

"All units respond," the reply crackles back. "Secure the perimeter."

Perfect.

I tap my earpiece. "Tank, secondary target."

A moment later, the sprinkler system kicks in, sending water cascading through the building.

I hear cursing as the guards scramble to protect their electronics.

"Lee, you're up."

I watch Lee slip through the emergency exit, using the chaos as cover. The guards are too busy dealing with the water and power loss to notice one more shadow among many.

"Two minutes," I murmur into my comm. "Get our boy and get out."

The security team has split up—two checking the power box, one circling the building's perimeter, the last trying to coordinate from his position by the front door. Their training works against them now. They are following protocol, maintaining formation, when they should be adapting.

Amateur hour.

A grunt of pain comes through my earpiece, followed by Lee's whispered, "Found him. Moving to exit point charlie."

I shift position, getting eyes on their escape route. "Tank, light it up."

The construction floodlights on the opposite side of the site suddenly blaze to life, powered by the generator we'd set up hours ago. The guards spin toward the new threat, momentarily blinded.

In that instant, two figures slip from the building's shadow into the tree line.

"We're clear," Lee's voice is barely a whisper.

"Prospects, fade out," I order. "Tank, kill the lights in thirty. Everyone roll to point beta. Do not engage."

One by one, my team confirms they are moving. I wait until Tank kills the floodlights before melting into the darkness myself.

The guards are still scrambling, trying to figure out what hit them. By the time they sort out their systems, we'll be long gone.

We regroup at the abandoned gas station two blocks away. Axel is soaked from the sprinklers but grinning, a thick folder tucked into his jacket.

"Worth it?" I ask.

His grin widens. "Oh yeah. I found who's bankrolling this little escapade."

"Do tell."

Before he can elaborate, my phone buzzes to life as I power it back on. Seventeen missed calls. Voice mails. Texts.

My blood runs cold as I read the messages.

> ANDI
>
> Hawk, I need help. Abby's got a fever and she won't stop coughing.
>
> ANDI
>
> We're in an ambulance, she's turning blue.
>
> ANDI
>
> Answer your fucking phone!
>
> ANDI
>
> We're at the hospital. She's in ICU.
>
> ANDI
>
> Don't bother calling. I've got it handled.

The last message is from Ginger.

GINGER

> I get it, Hawk. Club business comes first.
> But not like this. Andi and that baby
> needed you tonight, and you left her to
> go in that ambulance alone. You better
> pray that baby is okay, asshole. Because
> if anything happens to her, Andi will never
> forgive you.

"Fuck," I breathe, already moving to my bike.

"Hawk?" Lee calls after me. "We need to—"

"Handle it," I snap, kickstarting my engine. "I've got somewhere I need to be."

But even as I roar through the pre-dawn streets, I know it's too late.

I'd made my choice. I'd put the club first.

And for the first time in my life—that was the wrong fucking choice.

16

ANDI

I sit in the uncomfortable plastic chair beside Abby's bed, watching my tiny niece—my daughter in every way that matters—breathe with the help of an oxygen mask. Her dark curls are damp with sweat, her little chest rising and falling rapidly.

Croup, they'd said. A bad case that had come on suddenly in the middle of the night.

I run my thumb over her small, soft hand, my chest tightening as panic gnaws at the edges of my composure. I'd woken up to her choking cough, the sound so sharp and unfamiliar it sliced straight through the fog of sleep. There hadn't been time to think—only to act. I'd grabbed the kids, bundled them into my car, and driven to the hospital in nothing but sweatpants and adrenaline.

We'd had to pull over halfway there, her lips blue. I'd held her, trying to keep all three kids calm while waiting for an ambulance. An ambulance that finally came to take us all the way.

The clubhouse had been empty. Hawk was nowhere, the prospects had scattered to God knows where, and I'd been alone.

Again.

Just like always.

I should've been used to it by now—should've known that, when things fell apart, no one would be there to catch me.

That is the hardest part to admit, the thing that burns hot and unforgiving in my chest. I can't rely on anyone. I never have been able to, not really. It doesn't matter how much they promise, how many sweet lies they whisper when the world is quiet and the sky is dark.

When it comes down to it, I am the one who has to hold everything together, the one who has to keep Abby safe.

And I will.

Because I have no other choice.

I've always handled things myself. It looks like it's time to admit that the last few weeks have been a blip. A false sense of security.

I won't make that mistake again.

Amy is curled up asleep in the chair beside me, exhausted from crying. Adam dozes in his carrier at my feet. Four AM and I am alone with three kids in a hospital, one of them fighting to breathe.

I'd called him. God help me, I'd called him over and over, convinced he'd see my messages and swoop in light a knight in shining armor.

God, I am pathetic.

Club business had come first. Just like it always will.

"Hey." Ginger appears in the doorway, two cups of terrible hospital coffee in her hands. "Any change?"

I shake my head, accepting a cup. "The doctor dropped by and said the steroids are helping. Her oxygen levels are better."

"That's good." She perches on the arm of my chair, her hand settling on my shoulder. "Steel's outside if you need anything."

I manage a weak smile. The prospect had shown up an hour after we'd arrived, stationed himself in the hallway like a guard dog. He'd even managed to find a stuffed unicorn in the gift shop for Amy.

"Tell him he's off duty," I say, turning away. "We don't need a watchdog."

"Oh, honey." Ginger squeezes my shoulder. "Steel's not here as a prospect. He's here because he cares about these kids. And you."

I swallow hard against the lump in my throat. "I shouldn't have waited. I should have brought her in as soon as I heard her coughing. But I thought... I thought I could handle it."

And the medical bills. Insurance hasn't added them yet. I have no idea how I'll pay for this—or for the tests they'd had to run on Amy and Adam.

God, this could financially ruin us.

"You did handle it. You got her here. She's getting better."

I swallow. "But what if—"

"No what ifs." Her voice is firm. "She's going to be fine. And you're not alone."

Except I am. Because the one person I'd started to believe would be there for me is still missing in action.

"I can't do this anymore," I whisper.

"Do what?"

"Pretend." I gesture vaguely. "Pretend we're a family. Pretend he cares. Pretend any of this is real."

"Andi—"

"No." I straighten in my chair, decision crystallizing. "I need to stop lying to myself. These kids need stability. They need someone they can count on, not..." I trail off, the words stuck in my throat.

"And you don't think Hawk is that someone?" Ginger's voice is gentle. "Everyone makes mistakes."

"Yeah." I watch Abby's chest rise and fall. "But not everyone has three kids who need them."

She is silent.

"I need you to do me a favor," I say quietly.

"Name it."

"Can you have Steel help me move our stuff back to the house? While Hawk's still out?"

She's quiet for a long moment. "You sure about this?"

"No." I manage a weak laugh. "But I'm sure I can't watch my kids get hurt waiting for someone who's never going to put us first."

"Okay." She pulls out her phone. "I'll call in some help. We'll have you moved before sunrise."

I reach up, squeezing her hand where it still rests on my shoulder. "Thank you."

"Don't thank me yet." She stands, heading for the door. "This is going to hurt like hell before it gets better."

"I know." I turn back to Abby, watching her sleep. "But I'd rather hurt than keep hoping for something that's never going to happen."

Ginger pauses in the doorway. "He does care about you, you know."

"I know." My voice cracks slightly. "He just doesn't care enough."

She leaves me then, the soft sound of her boots fading down the hallway. In the quiet, I listen to the steady beep of monitors, to Amy's soft breathing, to Adam's occasional snuffle.

My kids. My responsibility. My choice.

When Hawk finally shows up—and he will, I know he will—I have to be strong enough to stick to that choice.

Even if it breaks what's left of my heart.

I must have dozed off in the uncomfortable hospital chair because the next thing I know, a rough hand is brushing hair from my face.

"Andi."

I jerk awake, disoriented until my eyes focus on Hawk crouching beside me. He looks rough—dusty leather, shadows under his eyes, worry etched into every line of his face.

Too little, too late.

"Don't touch me," I whisper, pulling away.

His hand drops. Behind him, Ginger gathers Adam who's begun fussing, her expression grim.

"Can we talk?" Hawk asks quietly. "Outside?"

I glance at Abby, sleeping peacefully now that her breathing has stabilized.

"I've got them," Ginger says softly. "Go."

The hallway is too bright, too sterile. I lean against the wall, exhaustion making my legs shake. Or maybe that's the anger.

God, looking at him hurts. There is so much anger in me. So much helpless fucking rage.

I am angry at him, at me, at this fear that won't quit.

"How is she?" Hawk asks.

"Now you care?"

"Of course I care—"

"No." I cut him off. "You don't get to do that. You don't get to show up now and act concerned when I called you seventeen times, and you couldn't be bothered to answer once."

"I was handling club business."

"And I was handling a baby who couldn't breathe!" The words come out as a harsh whisper. "She was turning blue, Hawk. Her lips were blue, and Amy was screaming, and Adam wouldn't stop crying, and I needed you. I fucking needed you."

He reaches for me. "Babe—"

"Don't." I step back. "Don't 'babe' me. I get it now. I see exactly where we stand in your priorities list."

"That's not fair. I didn't know—"

"Because you didn't pick up your fucking phone!" I laugh, the sound raw and far too broken. "You really want to talk about fair, Hawk? These kids have already had their parents abandon them. I won't let them go through that again."

"I made a mistake. I'm not abandoning anyone."

"No? Then where were you?" Each word feels like glass in my throat. "Where were you when I was begging them to help her breathe? When Amy wouldn't stop crying? When I had to make medical decisions alone?"

He flinches. "I'm here now."

"Yeah. Now. When your club business is handled." I wrap my arms around myself. "That's not good enough. We need someone who puts us first. We deserve that. Those kids deserve that."

Even if I don't.

"Andi, please—"

I step away from him. "I've already had Steel move our stuff back to the house."

He rears back. "You what?"

"You heard me." I lift my chin despite the tears burning the back of my throat. "I won't do this anymore. I won't let these kids think they come second. Not again."

"They don't—"

"They do. They always will." I swipe angrily at my eyes. "And that's fine. It's who you are. The club comes first. I knew that going in. I just... I thought..." I shake off the wishes I know better than to make. "But I was wrong."

"Don't do this." His voice is rough. "Let me explain. We can fix this."

"No. We can't." I turn toward the room. "Because next time it'll be the same thing. Club business will come up, and you'll have to choose, and it won't be us. It's never going to be us."

"Andi—"

I pause in the doorway. "For what it's worth, she's going to be okay."

"Andi, please, let me—"

"Goodbye, Hawk."

I walk away—back to my kids, back to the life I'd chosen. I don't look back.

I can't.

Because if I do, I might break. And I can't afford to break. Not when I have three kids who depend on me.

I have to do what is right. No matter how much my heart hurts.

17

ANDI

I pull into the driveway, trying to ignore the party happening across the street at the clubhouse. Music pulses through the night air as I check the rearview mirror. Abby's still wheezing slightly in her car seat, but we've been discharged–thank god. She has a follow up next week but all signs are good.

"Almost home, babies," I say, forcing cheer into my voice. "We'll have a bath then bed, I think."

Amy tugs at her car seat straps. "Tummy funny."

She's needed to go to the toilet since we left the hospital.

"I know, sweetie. Just hold on—"

"Wawy," she whimpers. "Tummy."

I'm already moving, scrambling to unbuckle her, but I'm not fast enough. She makes a tiny hiccuping sound and then—

Pink.

Pink *everywhere*.

The strawberry milk she'd insisted on having at the hospital cafeteria decorates her car seat, her clothes, and somehow manages to splash across both her sister and Adam.

For a moment, we all just stare at the carnage. Then Abby starts to scream, which sets off Adam.

"Ew! Ew! Ewwwwww!" Abby screams, holding her vomit covered shirt out.

Amy looks at me with huge eyes and says, "Oopsie."

The smell hits me a second later, a rancid scent of curled milk mixed with fries.

I gag, as Amy leans forward in her car seat and vomits all over the floor once more.

Galvanised into action, I leap out of the car, racing around to throw open Amy's door and haul her out.

The belt is slippery with vomit, and I find myself struggling to hit the button as Abby and Adam wail, and Amy stares up at me with big, sorrowful eyes.

I can't help it. I start laughing.

Maybe it's hysteria, maybe it's exhaustion, maybe it's the fact I'm standing in my driveway at midnight, covered in pink vomit while music talking about being in the club and getting nasty thumps from across the street.

Either way, the entire situation strikes me as hilarious.

The kids stop crying–seemingly startled by my breakdown.

Don't worry, I am too.

"Wawy?" Amy's lower lip trembles.

"It's okay, baby." I wipe tears—from laughter or stress, I'm not sure—from my eyes. "Sometimes tummies do funny things."

"Pink," Abby points out helpfully between coughs.

"Very pink," I agree, surveying the damage. Three kids, two car seats and a capsule, plus the car to clean up. By myself.

Perfect.

"More tummy," Amy announces, her expression panicked.

"Oh no—"

This time the pink milk hits my face and slides down my chest.

What kind of karma did I accrue in a previous life to deserve this?

"Inside," I declare, finally managing to unbuckle her car seat. "Everyone inside before anything else turns pink."

We make it halfway to the door before Adam spits up in solidarity with his sister.

I guess the family that sprays together, stays together.

It takes an hour to get everyone bathed and settled. An hour of tears, negotiations, and promises of a better tomorrow. Even Adam fights sleep, his tiny body wracked with hiccups from his crying jag.

Finally, *finally*, they're all clean and sleeping.

I strip the car seats, piling the covers into the washer before heading out to tackle the car itself. The night air is thick with humidity, and music still pounds from across the street as I dig through my cleaning supplies.

The smell of sour milk hits me as I open the back door. "Jesus."

Paper towels, cleaning spray, and determination–that's all I've got right now. I lean into the car, scrubbing at pink-tinged upholstery, trying not to gag.

Movement across the street catches my eye.

Hawk stands on his porch, illuminated by the party lights. Even from here, I can see the tension in his shoulders as he stares in my direction.

Our eyes meet.

For a moment, I think he might come over. That he might help, like he has so many times before.

Instead, he turns, heading for his bike.

The rumble of his engine is louder than the music as he rides away, leaving me alone with my pink-stained car and sleeping kids.

"Right," I mutter, turning back to my task. "This is what I wanted. To get rid of all the people I can't rely on."

I scrub harder at a particularly stubborn spot, ignoring the burning in my eyes.

As I finish cleaning, the baby monitor crackles with the sound of vomiting.

Rushing inside, I find Abby leaning over the side of her bed, missing the bucket I put beside it just for this.

"Oh, baby." I sweep her up, hurrying her into the bathroom as she begins to cry.

I want to weep alongside her.

I catch sight of myself in the mirror–I look exhausted, haggard.

I look like a single mom whose just spent the last three days in the hospital with her kid.

You've done hard things alone before, I silently tell myself as I hold Amy over the toilet, murmuring reassuring things to her. *You can do it again.*

I have to. I don't have any other choice.

18

HAWK

I am three bottles deep into trying to forget the look on Andi's face when Ginger finds me.

"Really?" She kicks an empty bottle aside. "This is your solution?"

I can't go home. Can't face the emptiness of the house, see her struggling with the kids across the street.

So I'd come to our bar. Owned by one crochety old-timer by the name of Devil, the bar has stood in this town for longer than the town existed. If a health inspector had dared to walk across the threshold, the place would have been shut down years ago. Instead, the bar—simply called 'Devil's' because it has no official name—still stands, slinging alcohol at all hours of the day and night, and serving food that tastes solely of grease and salt.

"Fuck off," I growl, pouring myself another whiskey.

"Charming." She perches on the bar seat beside me, watching me drain the shot. "You know what your problem is?"

"Don't care."

"Your problem," she continues as if I hadn't spoken, "is that you're so busy being sergeant-at-arms that you forgot how to be human."

I snort. "That right?"

"Yeah." Tank's voice joins in as he and Axel appear in the doorway. "That's right."

Great. An intervention.

"The club needed me," I growl.

"Bullshit." Axel drops into a chair. "I was fine. Could have waited it out or found another way out. You just didn't want to choose."

"Choose what?"

"Between the club and them." Ginger's voice is sharp. "Because if you chose them, it meant admitting you care. That they matter. That you might actually need someone."

"I don't need—"

"A family?" Tank cuts in. "People who love you? Yeah, you do. We all do."

"Those kids adored you," Ginger adds. "And that woman? She was falling for you. Hard."

"Was," I echo. The past tense hurts more than I want to admit.

"You know what I saw in that hospital?" Ginger's voice softens. "I saw a woman terrified for her kid. And instead of being able to lean on the man she trusted, she had to handle it alone. And no one can tell me that's the first time she's ever had to do anything alone."

"I didn't know—"

"You knew." Tank's tone is blunt. "You saw those calls coming in. You chose to ignore them."

"The club—"

"Stop hiding behind the club." Axel's usually gentle voice has an edge. "The club's family. Family means having each other's backs. All of us."

"Including those kids," Tank adds. "Who, by the way, are probably going to end up family anyway once Duck adopts Andi officially."

That pulls me up short. "What?"

"You didn't notice?" Ginger laughs. "Duck's been playing proud papa for months. Why do you think he gave her the restoration department? Man's looking for an heir, and his own kids aren't interested."

"Shit."

"Yeah, shit." She kicks my boot. "So congratulations. You just screwed up with the future queen of the garage."

"I fucked up," I whisper.

"Yeah, you did." Axel's voice is gruff. "Question is, what are you gonna do about it?"

"Nothing to do. She made her choice."

"Because you made yours first." Ginger slides off the stool. "You know what's sad? She wasn't asking you to choose between her and the club. She just wanted to know she mattered too."

"She does matter."

"Then fucking show her," Tank growls. "Because right now? All you're showing is that you're a coward."

"I'm not—"

"Prove it." Ginger heads for the door. "But first, sober up and have a shower. Those kids deserve better than a drunk biker trying to win back their mom."

She leaves me with that truth bomb, Tank following after shooting me a disappointed look.

Axel slides onto the seat beside me. "What's the plan?"

"I don't know," I admit. "I never signed up for this. Never thought I'd have someone like her."

"Yeah, I feel that." He picks up the whiskey bottle, swishing the liquid around. "Lucky fucker."

I shoot him a look. "The hell are you bitching about?"

"Nothing." He takes a long draw from the bottle then swipes his mouth with the back of his hand.

"Oh, this should be good." Lee's voice cuts through the bar as he and Stone enter. "Axel giving relationship advice or seeking it?"

"Shut it," Axel growls, hunching his shoulders.

Stone's laugh is low and rich. "He tell you about the traffic guard yet? "

I raise an eyebrow as Axel's face reddens. "No?"

"The hot brunette," Lee explains with unholy glee. "What was her name again? Rachel?"

"Poppy," Axel mutters.

"Right. Poppy." Lee's grin widens. "Button Road's closed and this fucker thinks he can glower his way past her. Not a chance."

"Fuck all of you." Axel stands, but there's no heat in it. "At least I didn't let the best thing in my life walk away because I was too scared to admit I needed her."

They sober, each turning to look at me.

His words hit like a punch to the gut.

"I put the club first."

Stone rolls his eyes. "Those kids and that woman are club. They're family, Hawk. We understand when shit—especially health shit—hits the fan. You've got our back, you need to trust that we'll have yours."

I swallow, nodding slowly.

"You can fix this," Stone says. "If you're willing to do the work."

"How?"

"By showing up," Lee replies. "Every day. Even when it's hard. Even when the club needs you. You find a way to do both—ask for help, explain it to her."

I think about Abby in that hospital bed. About Amy's tears. About the way Andi had looked at me like she'd been expecting me to let her down.

And I had.

But I don't have to keep letting them down.

"I need to go," I say finally.

"Yeah?" Axel's smile is knowing. "Got a plan?"

I stand, suddenly clear-headed despite the whiskey. "Yeah. I do."

"This should be good," Lee mutters.

But I am already moving, purpose driving me forward. Because for the first time since I'd watched Andi walk away, I know exactly what I need to do.

I just hope I'm not too late.

19

ANDI

The pounding on my front door matches the pounding in my head.

"Go away," I croak, but whoever it is can't hear me from the bathroom floor where I've been camping out for the last hour.

Adam's pitiful cries echo from his crib in the next room, while Amy's occasional sleepy whimpers remind me I have another sick baby to tend to. Only Abby has been spared so far, though her croup cough still rattles in her chest.

The pounding continues.

I try to push myself up, but my arms shake too much. Whatever stomach bug Amy picked up at the hospital, she's shared it with devastating efficiency.

A crash from the front of the house has me jerking

upright, instantly regretting the movement as my stomach rolls.

"Andi?" Hawk's voice carries down the hall. "Where are you?"

"No," I moan. "Not now."

But heavy boots are already heading my way, following the sound of retching children.

He appears in the bathroom doorway, filling the frame with his massive shoulders. One look at me on the floor and his expression darkens.

"Jesus, babe."

"What are you doing here?" I try to ask, the sound rough from my aching throat.

"Looking after what's mine." He crouches down beside me, gently tucking a stray, limp hair behind my ear. "You doing okay?"

"We're not yours," I protest weakly. I try to summon the energy to get up, to stand, to walk him to the door and kick his ass to the curb.

My stomach decides to lurch instead. I twist, more bile coming up.

He holds my hair as I heave, emptying whatever is left in my stomach.

"Here, little lamb. I got you." He hands me water to rinse my mouth and a damp cloth. He smells of cologne and leather, and looks like a million bucks.

"You should go."

"Mmhmm. Just as soon as I get you into bed."

Adam's cries grow louder, joining Amy's whimpers and my rolling stomach in a symphony of misery.

"They need me." I try to stand again.

"They've got me." He crouches beside me, one large hand settling on my forehead. "You're burning up."

"I'm fine."

"Sure you are." He scoops me up before I can protest, carrying me to my bedroom. "Stay put. I'll handle the kids."

"Hawk—"

"Stay." His tone brooks no argument. "Let me take care of you. All of you."

I want to argue. Want to tell him we don't need him. But Amy chooses that moment to start crying in earnest, and my stomach lurches again.

He is already moving, heading for the kids' room with purpose. I hear him murmuring to Amy, his voice low and soothing. A moment later, Adam's cries quiet too.

I must have dozed because the next thing I know, Hawk is back with water and crackers.

"Small sips," he orders, helping me sit up. "Amy's sleeping. Adam too. Abby's watching cartoons with some juice."

His hand supports my back as I sip the water, strong and steady. He's shed his cut, and his white T-shirt stretches across his shoulders as he leans in to check my temperature again.

"How did you know?" I ask, letting him take the glass. "That we were sick?"

"Duck." He sets the water aside, his hand lingering on mine. "He was worried when you didn't answer his texts about work. Said you never miss checking in."

"You had him spying on me?"

"No." His voice is soft. "He cares about you. All of us do."

I close my eyes against a fresh wave of nausea. "I can't do this right now."

"Do what?"

"This. Us. The conversation we need to have."

"I know." His thumb traces circles on my palm. "I'll be here until you're better, then we can work through what we need to."

I close my eyes, exhausted by the thought of arguing. "Until the next time the club needs you?"

His hand tightens on mine. "I fucked up. I know that. But I'm learning."

"Learning what exactly?"

He brushes hair from my face. "That being strong doesn't mean being alone. The club is family, Andi. And I should have asked them to look after what needed doing rather than ghosting you when you needed me."

I want to argue. Want to tell him it's too late. But his touch is so gentle and cool against my flushed skin.

"I called in reinforcements." He nods toward the hallway where I can hear Ginger's voice mixing with TV sounds. "Steel's making a pharmacy run. Duck's bringing soup."

"Duck doesn't make soup."

His smile is soft. "No, but Maggie does. And she's been wanting an excuse to mother you for months."

Tears prick my eyes. "We don't need—"

"Yeah, you do." He sits on the edge of the bed, his hand cool against my cheek. "And that's okay. Everyone needs help sometimes."

"Not me." But even as I say it, I know I'm lying.

"Especially you." His thumb brushes away a tear I hadn't realized had fallen. "Let me be here, Andi. Let me prove I can be what you need."

"And what's that?"

He leans in, pressing his forehead to mine. "Someone who puts his family first."

Family.

The word hits like a punch to the gut.

I want to argue. Want to hold on to my anger and hurt.

But I am so tired. So damn tired of doing everything alone.

"I can't do this right now," I whisper.

He presses a kiss to my forehead. "Then don't. Rest. I've got this."

And the thing is? I believe him.

I sigh, closing my eyes.

"This doesn't mean I forgive you."

His chuckle is low and filled with bitterness. "Don't worry, I have yet to forgive myself."

I want to ask what he means, but exhaustion pulls me under. I drift off, listening to him moving through the house, taking care of our kids, making things right.

Our kids.

The thought follows me into sleep, warm and terrifying and right.

ANDI

"We need to talk."

I look up from where I am folding laundry on the couch to find Hawk in the doorway. The kids are finally asleep after another long day of illness, but the house finally has that peaceful quiet that only comes after dark.

He's been here all week, sleeping on the couch, taking care of us while we fought off the stomach bug. Never complaining about the sick or the laundry or the stench. He is there.

Steady. Present. Patient.

It terrifies me how easily he's slipped back into our lives.

"Yeah," I agree, setting aside one of Adam's tiny shirts. "We do."

I've put off this talk for as long as possible, but we need to hash it out. He needs to understand where I am, and what I need if he really does want to make this work.

And I have a sneaky suspicion he does.

He sits beside me, closer than necessary but not quite touching. "I'm not going to promise I'll never let you down."

That isn't what I'd expected him to lead with.

"No?"

"No." He turns to face me fully. "Because sometimes I will. Sometimes the club will need me, and I'll have to go. Sometimes I'll make the wrong choice. I'm not perfect, Andi."

"I never asked you to be perfect."

"I know." His hand finds mine, warm and callused. "I'm sorry I wasn't there when you and Abby needed me."

"I was terrified," I whisper. "She was blue. I thought she was dying. I needed you."

His head bends and he brushes his lips over my knuckles. "You'll never know how sorry I am for leaving you to deal with that. So fucking sorry." His fingers lace with mine. "I could promise that will never happen again, but I can't. Shit happens, and sometimes no matter how much we fight, we let the people in our lives down."

His gaze pierces mine, direct and full of emotion.

"But I can promise to try. I want to be the man these kids deserve. The man you deserve."

"Hawk—"

"Let me finish." His other hand comes up to cup my cheek. "I've been thinking about what family means. Not just blood or patches, but the kind you choose."

My heart thunders against my ribs. "And?"

"I choose you. All of you." His thumb brushes my cheek. "I want to be here for middle-of-the-night fevers and first steps and Christmas mornings. I want to teach the girls to ride bikes and show Adam how to throw a punch. I want to fall asleep beside you every night and wake up to tiny humans jumping on our bed."

Tears burn my eyes. "You can't just—"

"I can. I am." His voice roughens. "I love you, Andi. I love our kids. And I'm going to spend every day proving it."

"Even when the club needs you?"

"We'll figure it out." He presses his forehead to mine. "I've already talked to Stone about stepping back from some duties. Delegating more to the prospects and other brothers."

That surprises me. "You'd do that?"

"For my family? Yeah." His smile is soft. "Turns out being sergeant-at-arms isn't worth much if I don't have anyone to come home to."

"I'm scared," I admit.

"Of what?"

"To believe you. To let myself need you." My voice cracks. "But I'm so tired of being alone. I missed you."

The admission costs me something, scraping raw against my pride. I've spent so long being strong, being enough by myself that to be with someone else feels like cracking my chest open and laying my heart bare.

"God, I missed you too." His arms tighten around me. "Every morning I'd wake up reaching for you."

"It's scary," I whisper into his shirt. "How much I want this to work. How much I need you."

He pulls back just enough to meet my eyes. "Say it again."

"I need you." The words come easier this time. "And that terrifies me because everyone I've ever needed has left. They all walked away. And I can't—" My voice breaks. "I can't watch you walk away again. Not when the kids love you. Not when I—"

"When you what?" His thumb traces my cheek, catching tears I hadn't realized were falling.

"I love you." The words tumble out, unstoppable now. "I love how you make pancakes shaped like dinosaurs. How you know which of the twins is which even when they try to trick you. How Adam lights up when he hears your bike. How you make me feel safe enough to be scared sometimes."

"Andi—"

"No, let me finish." I press my hand to his chest, feeling his heart thunder under my palm. "I love you. And it scares the hell out of me because for the first time in my life, I want to let someone help carry the load. I want to believe in someone else's strength besides my own."

His forehead presses to mine, his breath warm against my lips. "Then believe in me. Believe in us. I'll spend every day proving we're worth the risk."

"Promise?"

"With everything I am." He kisses me then, soft and sweet and full of promise. "You and these kids? You're everything."

I wipe at my wet cheeks. "You're taking three kids with this deal."

His tone leaves no room for argument. "If you'll have me, then I swear I'll spend the rest of my life being worthy of your trust, and theirs."

I study his face, seeing the truth there. The love. The determination.

"When you mess up, I'll be mad," I say softly.

"Justifiably so."

"I'll make you do laundry. And change all of Adam's diapers."

His lips quirk. "You'll have every right to be."

"But you'll come home?"

"Always." He pulls me closer. "No matter what, I'll always come home to you."

I let myself lean into him, let myself believe. "Okay."

"Okay?" His voice holds hope.

"Yeah." I press my face into his neck, breathing in leather and soap and him. "But you're still sleeping on the couch."

His laugh rumbles through his chest. "Can I convince you otherwise?"

"You can try."

His smile turns wicked. "Challenge accepted."

He kisses me then, slow and deep, like he's trying to memorize the taste of me. His hands slide into my hair, angling my head to deepen the kiss as he pulls me closer.

This is different from our other kisses. Those have been charged with need or desperation.

This feels like coming home.

"Missed you," he murmurs against my lips. "Missed this."

"Show me," I whisper.

He pulls back just enough to meet my eyes, his own dark with intent. Then he stands, scooping me into his arms in one smooth motion.

"What are you doing?"

"Taking you to bed." He starts down the hall. "Unless you object?"

I wrap my arms around his neck, pressing a kiss to his jaw. "The kids—"

"Are out cold." He shoulders open my bedroom door. "And I've got the baby monitor right here."

He lays me on the bed with surprising gentleness, following me down until his weight presses me into the mattress.

"Still want me on the couch?" he asks, his lips trailing down my neck.

"Hmm." I arch into him as his hands find skin. "I might be persuaded to reconsider."

His laugh is low and rich. "I was hoping you'd say that."

Then his mouth is on mine again, and words become unnecessary. His tongue sweeps into my mouth as his hands slide under my shirt, callused fingers mapping the curve of my spine. I arch into his touch, wanting more, needing everything he can give me.

We take our time undressing each other, each revealed inch of skin a revelation. His tattoos are a roadmap I explore with fingers and tongue, tracing tiny kisses over the club's emblem on his chest, feeling his heart thunder under my lips.

There's no rush here, no pressure. Time seems to stand still as we rediscovered each other, relearning what it takes to make the other shiver with pleasure.

"Missed this," he murmurs, his mouth trailing slow, delicious kisses down my neck. "Missed you. The way you taste, the sounds you make."

His hands find my breasts, thumbs brushing over sensitive peaks until I'm gasping. When he replaces his fingers with his mouth, the wet heat of his tongue has me arching off the bed.

This is no longer gentle lovemaking—it's a reclaiming. A branding of one to the other. Each touch, each kiss, each shared breath is both an apology and a promise.

He works his way down my body with devastating focus, as if he's trying to memorize every curve, every reaction. His beard scrapes deliciously against my inner thigh as he settles between my legs.

"Look at me," he demands softly.

I prop myself up on my elbows, meeting his gaze. The intensity there steals my breath.

"God, you're beautiful," he breathes, his eyes dark with want and something deeper, something that makes my heart clench. "So fucking beautiful. Spread out for me, trusting me again."

"Hawk—"

"Let me show you," he whispers against my skin. "Let me prove how much I need you."

Then his mouth is on me, and coherent thought becomes impossible. He takes me apart with lips and tongue, working me higher and higher until I'm trembling on the edge.

But it's not enough. I need more. Need *him*.

I pull him back up my body, desperate for his kiss, his touch, the solid weight of him above me. His hands and mouth work magic on my body, drawing sounds from me I didn't know I could make.

"Tell me you're mine," he growls against my throat.

"I'm yours," I gasp. "Always yours."

His cock slides home, and we both groan as he fills me. The stretch and burn of him is exquisite, dancing me across a knife edge of pleasure and pain. His body covers mine completely, his weight a delicious anchor as he holds himself still, letting me adjust.

"I love you, Andi. So fucking much."

His mouth finds my breast, teeth grazing sensitive flesh as his thumb works circles against my clit.

My answer is to lift my hips and beg for more, wrapping my legs around him to pull him deeper. His groan rumbles through his chest as he begins to move, each thrust slow and deep like he's trying to claim every inch of me.

His free hand grips my hip hard enough to leave marks as he holds me in place, thrusting into me, claiming me, branding me.

"Mine," he growls, picking up his pace. "Say it again."

"Yours." I drag my nails down his back, loving how his muscles bunch under my hands. "All yours."

His rhythm falters at my words, his control slipping.

Good. I want him as desperate as I feel, as consumed by this need between us.

"Never letting you go again," he promises, his voice rough. Each word is punctuated by a thrust that drives me higher. "I love you."

The raw honesty in his voice, combined with the perfect angle of his hips, sends me over the edge. I shatter around him, my body clamping down as wave after wave of pleasure crashes through me. He follows a moment later, my name a promise on his lips as he pulses inside me.

After, he holds me close, his fingers drawing gentle patterns across my skin. The silence between us is easy, even if it holds an unasked questions.

I sigh, closing my eyes, knowing we've crossed a line. There's no going back from this. From us.

Smiling, I open my eyes, turning my head toward him.

"Stay," I whisper into the darkness.

His arms tighten around me. "Forever, little lamb."

EPILOGUE 1

HAWK

"Those papers we found," Lee says, leaning against the porch pole. "Cash has been pouring over them. Summit made a mistake."

I raise an eyebrow in question.

"There was one transaction—a small one, but he traced it. It's cartel."

"Damn." I shake my head. "What are they up to?"

"No idea. But speaking of what someone's up to." Lee nods across the road to where Axel is tinkering in the clubhouse garage with his bike. "He's riding past that hot traffic controller three times this week. Think he knows we're on to him?"

I follow his gaze across the street to the clubhouse. Andi and I have moved into her former rental after purchasing the place from her landlord. It's conveniently located close enough to the Clubhouse that I can still fulfill my duties, and oversee anything the club needs.

The road captain has been finding excuses to ride that route ever since the new traffic guard started. Something about her has caught his attention, though he refuses to share.

"Let him be," I say, remembering how it feels to be caught off guard by unexpected feelings.

Speaking of. Andi comes outside, a strange expression on her face, her cell held limply in one hand.

"Everything okay?" I ask quietly.

She glances up at me, a strange mix of emotions crossing her face. "Can I talk to you?"

I leave Lee, following Andi inside our house and down into the bedroom. She shuts the door, locking it.

A tingle of apprehension snakes up my spine.

I pull her in, holding her close. "What's happened?"

"Amanda called."

My body goes rigid. "And?"

"She signed them. The papers. All of them."

My world stops. "She what?"

"Signed over her parental rights." Andi's voice cracks. "We can officially adopt our kids."

My throat feels tight. I open my mouth to speak, but feel the words get caught.

I'm fucking devastated for my kids that their mother could discard them so easily. But one look at Andi and I know Amanda's made the right choice. Those kids will never want for love in their life.

My woman watches me, her gaze searching my face. "That's if you still want—"

I cut her off with a kiss.

"Always," I promise against her lips. "They were always ours."

She smiles, tears in her eyes. "Yeah?"

"Yeah." I pull her closer. "Though, if we're making that official, I figure we should do the same."

I begin backing her up toward our chest of drawers.

Her breath catches. "What do you mean?"

I've been waiting for the perfect moment—knowing I need to give her a little slice of the joy she's brought into my life.

Now seems the perfect time.

I pull a drawer open, digging out the small box I'd purchased weeks ago. "Marry me, Andi."

Her breath catches, her eyes widening.

I'm not asking.

"Hawk—"

"Marry me," I repeat, opening the box to reveal a diamond and sapphire ring. "Be my wife."

She stares at the ring, then at me. "You planned this?"

"Been planning it since you forgave me." I take her hand. "Just waiting for the right moment."

Her smile could light up the night. "Yes."

"Yes?"

"Yes." She pulls me down for another kiss. "A thousand times yes."

She jumps into my arms, and I walk backward, kissing her all the way to our bed where I'll make sweet, slow love to her.

A cry sounds down the hall, both of us freezing in place. It's followed a second later by twin squeals.

Chuckling, Andi pulls back, sliding slowly down my body.

"We can celebrate later," she murmurs, kissing me one final time. "Come on, let's go tell our kids."

I can't think of anything—except watching Andi come—that I'd rather do.

EPILOGUE 2

HAWK

"Hold still, princess," I murmur, trying to wrangle Amy's dark curls into something resembling the hairstyle Ginger had demonstrated.

"Pitty," she declares, touching the white flowers woven through her sister's already-done hair.

"Very pretty," I agree. Both girls wear matching white dresses, looking like tiny angels. If angels wear combat boots under their dresses because they refuse any other footwear.

Just like their mother.

A knock at the door has me looking up to find Duck, Adam perched on his hip. The baby wears a tiny leather vest over his dress clothes, matching the ones the girls had insisted on wearing over their dresses. They're all branded with the new insignia, which matches the cuts Duck handed out proudly earlier that week.

"You ready?" Duck asks. "Your bride's getting antsy."

My heart skips. "She okay?"

"Nervous as hell." His eyes crinkle. "But happy. Real happy."

I finish Amy's hair, pressing a kiss to her forehead. "There. Perfect."

"Go," Duck says, somehow managing to wrangle all three kids. "I've got them. You've got somewhere to be."

The clubhouse has been transformed. Lights twinkle everywhere, white flowers softening the usual rough edges. Bikes line the lot, their chrome gleaming in the setting sun.

I take my place at the front of the aisle, fidgeting as I wait for the crowd to hush. Music begins to play, people rise from the seats, and all I see is Andi.

She appears in the doorway on Duck's arm, and my world stops. Her dress is simple, white lace that hugs her curves before flowing to the ground. But it's her smile that knocks me breathless.

The twins precede her down the aisle, tossing flower petals everywhere except the walkway. Adam, carried by Ginger, waves his tiny fist at everyone he passes, flashing his gummy smile at their attention.

Then Andi is there, taking my hand, and nothing else matters.

We'd written our own vows. Simple promises we intend to keep.

"I promise to always come home to you," I say, sliding the ring onto her finger.

"I promise to let you help carry the load," she replies, her voice shaking slightly as she gives me my ring.

The party afterward descends into chaotic delight, bikes revving, kids running everywhere, music and laughter filling the night. The twins dance with Steel while Adam is passed from arms to arms, collectively making the entire club fall in love with him.

"Happy?" I ask, pulling Andi close as we watch our family celebrate.

"Perfect," she says, leaning into me. "Though I think Abby just convinced Axel to let her sit on his bike."

I glance over to where our daughter is indeed climbing onto the enforcer's prized Harley, her dress hitched up to her knees.

"Should we stop her?"

Andi laughs. "Nah. She's got him wrapped around her finger almost as bad as you."

"Like mother, like daughter."

She turns in my arms, pressing close. "I love you."

"Love you too, little lamb." I kiss her soft and sweet. "Always will."

Around us, the party rages on. Our crazy, beautiful, mixed-up family celebrating in the only way we know how.

Loud, chaotic, and full of love.

Fucking perfect.

Thanks for reading!
Why not dive into the next in the Stoneheart MC Series
with Megan Wade's Hard as Stone featuring Axel and a
certain traffic controller....

Want more?
Check out EvieMitchell.com

ABOUT EVIE MITCHELL

Fierce Romance
Evie Mitchell is a thirty-something romance author
(she/her/hers) who loves tales of fierce romance.
She lives with a chronic illness and often writes
disability-inclusive romance.
Her loves include steamy romance novels, her husband,
their THREE sausage dogs (heaven help her), and her
ever-growing collection of book-related mugs.

You can catch Evie at the below.

Join Evie's reader group:
https://www.facebook.com/groups/EvieMitchells
GreedyReaders

Follow Evie on all socials
@EvieMitchellAuthor

Visit Evie's website for her current booklist:
www.EvieMitchell.com

ALSO BY EVIE MITCHELL

All Access Series

Knot My Type

Love Flushed

Darn Knit All

Larsson Siblings

Thunder Thighs

Clean Sweep

The X-List

Reality Check

The Christmas Contract

The A-List

Capricorn Cove

The Shake-up

Double the D

Muffin Top

The Mrs. Clause

New Year, Knew You

Double Breasted

As You Wish

You Sleigh Me

Meat Load

Resolution Revolution

Dogg Pack

Puppy Love

Bad English

The Frock Up

Pier Pressure

Trick or Trent

New Year's Faye

Reigning Hearts

The Marriage Claim

Silent Knight

Men of Trinity Bay

Kink in the Road

Nameless Souls MC

Runner

Wrath

Ghost

Shield

Elliot Security

Rough Edge

Bleeding Edge

www.ingramcontent.com/pod-product-compliance
Lightning Source LLC
Chambersburg PA
CBHW010434170726
48283CB00011B/3212